The
LAST
of
the HIGH
KINGS

Also by Kate Thompson:

The Switchers Trilogy
Switchers
Midnight's Choice
Wild Blood
The Switchers Trilogy
(3 in 1)

The Missing Link Trilogy
The Missing Link
Only Human
Origins

The Beguilers
(CBI Bisto Award 2002)

The Alchemist's Apprentice
(CBI Bisto Award 2003)

Annan Water
(CBI Bisto Award 2005)

The New Policeman
(Guardian Fiction Prize 2005,
Whitbread Children's Book Award 2005,
Dublin Airport Authority Children's Book
Award 2005 and CBI Bisto Award 2006)

The Fourth Horseman

The LAST of the HIGH KINGS

KATE THOMPSON

THE BODLEY HEAD
London

THE LAST OF THE HIGH KINGS
A BODLEY HEAD BOOK
Hardback: 978 0 370 32925 3
Trade paperback: 978 0 370 32926 0

Published in Great Britain by The Bodley Head,
an imprint of Random House Children's Books

This edition published 2007

1 3 5 7 9 10 8 6 4 2

Copyright © Kate Thompson, 2007

The Random House Group Limited makes every effort to ensure
that the papers used in its books are made from trees that have been
legally sourced from well-managed and credibly certified forests.
Our paper procurement policy can be found at:
www.randomhouse.co.uk/paper.htm

Addresses for companies within The Random House Group Limited
can be found at: www.randomhouse.co.uk/offices.htm

Set in 13.5/17pt AGaramond

RANDOM HOUSE CHILDREN'S BOOKS
61–63 Uxbridge Road, London W5 5SA

www.kidsatrandomhouse.co.uk

THE RANDOM HOUSE GROUP Limited Reg. No. 954009

A CIP catalogue record for this book is available from the British Library.

Printed and bound in Great Britain by
Mackays of Chatham plc, Chatham, Kent

For my mother, Dorothy Thompson.
Thanks for everything.

On top of the mountain stood a hill of stones. It measured one hundred paces around the base and twenty paces from the bottom to the top. Of all the people of the seven tribes there was no one who could remember when it had been built, but of all the people of the seven tribes there was no one who could not remember why.

On top of the hill of stones stood a boy. He was barely twelve years old but he considered himself a man, already a proven warrior and hunter. If the talks going on in his father's fort went well he would soon be married. If they went badly he would, even sooner, be dead.

The young man who stood beside him on the hill of stones was a cousin. He was short; barely taller than the boy, and some people said it was his small size that had made him so angry. He was the right man to go hunting with and the wrong man to have an argument with. He had killed stags and bears and men in close combat, and when he saw blood he always wanted to see more of it. But even he had not wanted to see this blood; the blood of his young cousin. It was with great reluctance that he had allowed himself to be persuaded to take on this watch.

Throughout the whole of the night the two of them had waited on the beacon, taking it in turns to rest, but never to sleep. A constant hard wind had been blowing against them but it hadn't been that which kept them awake. They were watching for a messenger to tell them that the boy would live or a sign to tell them he would die.

Time after time, throughout that longest of nights, the boy wondered what had compelled him to speak. His father, as everyone had known he would, had asked for a hero, and the words were barely out of his mouth before the boy had called out with his own name. He hadn't thought about it. Something in him that was quicker and deeper than thought had spoken. The meeting had exploded into uproar. A dozen men and women demanded to be chosen instead of the boy and the voice that shouted loudest and longest was that of the man who stood beside him now. But it was no use. Battling against his own powerful feelings, the boy's father had quelled the storm. It was he who would be leading the forthcoming negotiations. It was right that his own flesh and blood should pay the price if they failed.

The fort on the edge of the plain could not be seen from the beacon, which was why two signalmen had been stationed at the edge of the mountain top. Both the fort and the mountain's edge had brush pyres waiting to be lit if the talks broke down. The one at the fort would signal to the watchers on the mountain and theirs, in turn, would signal to the boy. All through the night he had stared in its direction, sometimes imagining he saw the red glow of fire or smelled the smoke from burning kindling. Now, as the day dawned, he could see the two men, more cousins, their backs turned towards him as they kept their careful watch upon the fort. In the daylight the fires would not be lit. There were other signals instead. Arms stretched up and held still for success and reprieve. Arms to the sides and then up, waving, for failure and death.

The boy wondered why it was all taking so long. Could they still be talking down there? Perhaps the meeting had finished hours ago and no one had thought of coming up to tell them. He sighed and stamped his sandalled feet in an effort to warm them.

'Hungry?' said his cousin.

'No.'

There was bread and cold meat in a hide bag but

neither of them had touched it all night. The boy rewrapped his cloak around him and fastened it with the gold pin that his mother had given him shortly before her death.

'You keep this,' he said. 'If—'

But the young man shook his head. 'If you die I will not be long coming after you. There are those who say I'm an angry man, but if I am made to spill your blood there isn't a beast in the forest nor a man among the seven tribes that will not know what my anger looks like.'

The boy shook his head. 'Don't take it out on them,' he said. 'They aren't to blame for this.'

But he saw, already, the glint of derangement in those dark brown eyes, and he realized that an early death had always been written on his cousin's brow. And at that same moment he saw that the same thing was written on his own. His death was waving at him from the horizon. He saw the signallers turn back and look towards the plain, then wave again, more urgently.

'Do it,' he told his cousin.

'Then say it.' The boy looked and saw tears streaming down his cousin's wind-burned face. He turned away from him and saw the signalmen running hard, in opposite directions, away from their unlit pyre.

Something was coming. Already. How could it all

have happened so fast? The boy found that his knees were shaking so hard that they would scarcely support his weight.

'I swear,' he began, but his voice was constricted by fear and it squeaked like a child's. The words would be worthless if he did not mean them.

The mountain was shaking. Huge, heavy feet were thundering up the hillside from the plain.

'Say it,' said his cousin.

Two enormous, monstrous heads appeared over the rim of the mountain top, then a third, then a fourth. The creatures had reached the top and were advancing on the beacon with massive strides, and they were far, far more terrible than he had ever imagined.

There was no more time. The boy took a deep breath and, as he did so, all doubt left him.

'I swear that I will guard this place,' he said, and his voice was clear and strong. 'I will stay here and guard it whether I am alive or dead.'

The beasts were almost upon them. Behind him, the boy heard the whistling swish of a sword being swung through the air with ferocious strength.

And for a short while afterwards, everything was very, very still.

NEW YEAR'S EVE

1

JJ Liddy stood in the hall and yelled at the top of his voice.

'Where's Jenny?'

The old house, which had been full of noise and activity, fell silent and still. JJ groaned, then shouted again.

'Has anybody seen Jenny?'

His wife, Aisling, came out of the sitting room. 'I thought you were watching her,' she said.

'Well, I was, a minute ago,' said JJ. 'Then I couldn't because she wasn't there.'

Aisling gave a martyred sigh. Their eldest, Hazel, appeared at the top of the stairs. 'She's not up here,' she said.

JJ went out into the yard. 'Jenny!' he yelled, trying to keep the irritation out of his voice. If she knew that he was angry she would never come. 'Jenny!'

She probably wouldn't come anyway. She rarely did.

JJ went back into the house and began searching for his walking boots. He found them underneath a pile of cased instruments which were waiting beside the door to be packed into the car, and as he was putting them on Donal came down the stairs with a half-filled backpack.

'Does that mean we aren't going, then?' he said. Donal was nine, and was by far the easiest of all Aisling and JJ's children. He seldom had much to say, and he never made a fuss about anything.

'Well, we can hardly go without her, can we?' said JJ, tugging at a bootlace.

'I don't see why not,' said Hazel, who was still at the top of the stairs, leaning on the banisters. 'I don't see why we have to let her ruin everything all the time.'

'Bold Jenny,' said Aidan, arriving on the scene with a hammer. He was nearly three, and going through an aggressive phase. Aisling and JJ spent a lot of their time trying to disarm him.

'She wouldn't care anyway,' Hazel went on. 'She doesn't want to hang around with the rest of us; that's why she's always swanning off on her own. She probably wouldn't even notice if we weren't here when she got back. She'd probably be delighted.'

'Oh, it doesn't matter,' said Aisling gloomily. 'We can always go in the morning.'

'It does matter,' said Hazel irritably. 'If we go in the

morning we'll miss the party, and that's the whole point.'

'I'll find her,' said JJ, lacing his second boot.

'Yeah, right you will,' said Hazel, stomping back to her bedroom.

JJ went out and shut the door behind him.

'Bold Daddy!' said Aidan, raising the hammer with both hands and aiming it at one of the glass panels in the door. Aisling snatched it out of his hand the instant before it hit the target and held it up high, out of his reach. He lunged at her and screamed, but she sidestepped and escaped into the kitchen. Silently, Donal retreated, leaving Aidan to finish his tantrum alone on the hallway floor.

As JJ crossed the field called Molly's Place he felt his annoyance subsiding. More than that, he found he could almost sympathize with Jenny. Although it was midwinter the weather was mild. A gentle breeze blew a soft, misty drizzle in from the sea, and the grey hills which rose ahead of him were inviting. Why would anyone want to squeeze into a crowded car and be stuck there for three hours when they could stride off into the fresh, earth-scented wilds beyond the farm?

He spotted something in the grass and changed his course. One of Jenny's shoes. It meant he was on the right track, at least. He looked up and caught a glimpse of something white on the mountainside far ahead. That big old goat again. It had been hanging around a lot lately, and it made JJ uneasy. He suspected that it might not be quite what it appeared to be. He suspected, as well, that Jenny was already a long, long way ahead. She hadn't got that much of a head start, he was fairly sure, but she was capable of moving incredibly quickly once she had, as she always did, jettisoned her shoes.

JJ looked at his watch. It was two o'clock, which meant that there were still about three hours of daylight left in which to find her. They wouldn't make it for dinner, but provided they were on the road by six they would still arrive in plenty of time for the party. His sister Marian had married an accordion player from Cork and their new year parties were famous in traditional music circles. They were one of the highlights of JJ's year, and the annual trip to Cork was just about the only time the whole family went away together. Everyone loved it and looked forward to it. Everyone, that was, except Jenny.

JJ found the other shoe just inside the boundary wall of the farm. That was good luck. More often than not only one would turn up, and Jenny's room was littered with shoes that had lost their partners.

'Jenny!'

Beyond the farm the land became much wilder. This

was the winterage that belonged to the Liddy farm, but unlike Mikey's land at the top of the mountain it had hardly any grazing at any time of year, and to a farmer it was useless. The rocky slopes rose steeply, and in hollows and gullies there were belts of woodland, mostly ash and hazel, guarded by blackthorn and brambles. There were plenty of places where Jenny could be hidden from view. She could be almost anywhere.

'Jenny!'

There was no answer. Even the white goat had disappeared. JJ sighed and, with a last glance back at the house, climbed over the dry-stone wall.

2

'Can I go to Ennis with the girls, then,' said Hazel, 'if Jenny's not back by six?'

'I suppose so,' said Aisling. It was nearly five already, and a few minutes earlier she had got up to turn on the outside light. This was not for JJ's benefit, or for Jenny's, but for Aidan, who had found three large pieces of polystyrene packaging in the shed and was out in the back yard, pulverizing them with a brick. It was making a terrible mess, which someone would have to clear up at some stage, but it was rare for anything to keep Aidan occupied for more than a couple of minutes at a time, and Aisling was reluctant to bring an end to the relative peace.

Hazel went off to phone her friends and book a seat on the bus. Aisling looked at the clock again. She would soon have to think about making a meal. There was hardly anything in the house, because they hadn't planned on being there that night. She could probably scrape something together with tins and frozen food, but the trouble was she didn't want to. She had been looking forward to getting away; to being fed for a change, and to mucking in with Marian and Danny in the big friendly kitchen down in Cork. She had been looking forward to sitting at the piano and having a few tunes tonight. But then Jenny . . .

A wave of anxiety washed over her thoughts and changed their direction. What were they going to do about her? The child had been a disaster right from the word go. She wasn't stupid or devious or nasty, she was just completely intractable. She spent most of her time roaming around the countryside and seemed to be incapable of doing as she was told. And recently it had got worse. Much worse.

At least, in the past, she had gone to school. She was now eleven, and although she still went occasionally, it was becoming the exception rather than the rule. Most mornings when Aisling and JJ got up, Jenny was already gone. And when she was gone, she was gone all day. The girl didn't seem to need the things that normal children did. She never took anything to eat, and she never came home for lunch. She wore light clothes, often forgetting to take a jacket, even in the foulest of weather. And although Aisling's notes to the teachers were full of them, the truth was that Jenny never ever got a cough or a cold or a sore throat. But it couldn't go on. The school principal was beginning to get suspicious and had starting asking questions that Aisling found difficult to answer. It should have been JJ's responsibility to deal with that kind of thing, but the trouble was that JJ was hardly ever there.

Because JJ Liddy, over the last few years, had become a household name. He had made four CDs and he spent a large part of every year touring at home and abroad, playing to packed houses wherever he went. That hadn't been the plan when they married. The deal had been that JJ would stay at home and make violins, and Aisling would go back to working as a homoeopath. They were supposed to be sharing the housework and the child-rearing, but as the years went by those things had become, almost exclusively, Aisling's department.

Anger simmered under her breastbone. She had put up with it for years, partly for the sake of JJ's career and partly because he was better paid for playing music than she would be for working as a homoeopath. But money wasn't everything. Aisling's life was passing her by, and Jenny's behaviour was the last straw. It was high time things began to change.

3

Aisling defrosted bread and made soup from frozen peas and tinned sweetcorn. It was just about ready when JJ came in with Aidan in his arms. They were both covered in tiny white polystyrene bubbles, and Aidan was still holding his brick.

'Out!' Aisling shouted, waving at the drifting trail of weightless particles. 'Get it off outside!'

But it was too late. With a dramatic flourish Aidan tossed a handful of bubbles into the air.

'Snowing!' he said gleefully.

Bits of polystyrene settled gently in the butter, the milk, the soup, and floated on to the hot-plate of the range, where they melted with a poisonous stench. Aisling downed tools and went to bed. She stayed there while JJ cleaned up the polystyrene, salvaged the soup, fed the three children who were present and carried the smallest one, kicking and screaming every inch of the way, up to bed.

Hazel overtook them on the stairs. 'I have to go in half an hour,' she said. 'Will you give me a lift to the village?'

'Why don't you stay in?' said JJ. 'We could have our own little party to ring in the new year.'

'Mum said I could go,' said Hazel.

If JJ had any objections she didn't wait to hear them, but went into her room and closed the door. She began selecting clothes from her drawers and wardrobe, but she wasn't actually going to change just yet. The custom was for all the girls to meet up and get dressed together. Half the clothes that Hazel put into her bag were ones she knew she wasn't going to wear. In fact, she might end up wearing none of her own clothes at all, since they were all endlessly borrowing and swapping. But it was still important to choose exactly the right things and pack them carefully. It was almost the best bit: a delicious appetizer for the evening that lay ahead.

Donal was watching the TV when Jenny came in.

'Don't you dare turn it off,' he said to her.

'Why?'

'Because I'm watching it, that's why.' He sat forward on the edge of the sofa so he could jump up and catch her if she tried to turn it off. She was two years older than him but he was already as tall as she was and considerably heavier. In any physical struggle he would have had the upper hand, but it never came to that. Not quite. She didn't turn off the TV now. Instead she sprawled on the sofa behind him. Her dress was soaked. Polystyrene bubbles from the yard clung to her bare feet and legs.

'Get changed,' said Donal.

'Why?'

'Because you're wet. Where have you been, anyway?'

'Out.'

'I know you've been out. You wrecked our new year.'

'Why?'

'Because we couldn't go to Cork. We missed the party.'

Jenny sat up and began rubbing the polystyrene off her feet and on to the carpet. 'I forgot,' she said. 'I was talking to the púca.'

'And how is the púca today?' said Donal sardonically.

'He's fine. He told me where there's a ghost.'

'A ghost as well?' said Donal. 'And what did the ghost have to say for itself?'

'I didn't see it,' said Jenny. 'I'll go there tomorrow.'

'No you won't,' said Donal. 'We're going to Cork tomorrow, and you'd better not forget this time.'

The phone rang. It was Marian, wondering what had happened to them.

While Donal explained, Jenny got up from the sofa and unplugged the TV. She couldn't think while that thing was blaring away, and she wanted to think now. She wanted to think about the ghost.

He was very sad and very lonely, the púca had told her. He had been there for thousands of years, watching over the beacon, and the púca had a plan to set him free. He wanted Jenny to go and talk to the ghost and make friends with him, but he didn't want her to tell him who had sent her. That part was a secret, the púca said, and if she gave it away then the rescue plan wouldn't work. Jenny had never had a secret before. She had never met a ghost before, either. Both things were exciting, but a little bit frightening as well. She lay back down on the sofa and thought about them.

As she was crossing the landing with her bag of clothes Hazel paused. The door to her parents' room was ajar and she could hear a tense conversation emerging. She sat down on the top step. Waiting, not eavesdropping. It wasn't her fault if she could hear every word they said.

Her mother was speaking.

'But it's all become such a mess, JJ. I don't know how we got into this state.'

'It's not the end of the world,' JJ said. 'We can still go in the morning.'

'I'm not talking about that!' said Aisling, her voice rising in frustration. 'I'm talking about the way we're living!' She waited for JJ to respond, and when he didn't she went on: 'It's just madness. I can't plan anything. Some days I can't even get out to the shops until Hazel comes home because Jenny has gone wandering off while I'm not looking.'

'I'll have another talk with her—' JJ began, but Aisling interrupted him with a snort of derision.

'Talk?' she said. 'You might as well sit down and have a talk with the cat. It would take about as much notice of you as Jenny does. It's a complete waste of time talking to her. It goes in one ear and straight out the other.'

'OK. But I don't know what else to do. Maybe we should get locks on all the doors. I mean the kind you can only open with a key. Then she couldn't get out.'

'I've thought of that,' said Aisling gloomily. 'I couldn't live with it. Can you imagine it, with four kids trying to come in and out? I'd be like a jailer.'

There was a long silence and Hazel was about to go in and remind them about her lift when Aisling began again.

'This was never the deal, JJ. I never volunteered to

be at home on my own for half the year while you sailed off around the world playing tunes.'

'I know, I know,' said JJ.

'The deal was that you'd be at home making fiddles and helping with the children. The deal was that I'd go back to work.'

'Well, you know the story as well as I do,' said JJ. 'I would be making fiddles if he had brought me that wood.'

'That's right,' said Aisling. 'He didn't bring the wood but we still have to keep our side of the agreement. How is that, JJ?'

Hazel waited to hear about the wood and who it was that ought to have delivered it, but the question seemed to have put an end to the conversation. She looked at her watch. It was 8.30. Time to go. She stood up and called out for a lift.

By the time JJ came back from taking Hazel to the village, Aisling had got up. She was sitting with Donal watching TV with the volume turned down low. Jenny was asleep on the sofa, underneath an old woollen blanket. The fire in the hearth was lit.

'We could have a tune, I suppose,' JJ said. 'Just the four of us. Nice and cosy.'

'Shh,' said Donal. 'Don't wake her up.'

'Maybe in a while,' said Aisling. 'It's early yet.'

24

JJ stared at the television, realizing he hated it almost as much as Jenny did. It reminded him of lonely hotel rooms from Berlin to Birmingham to Beijing. Aisling might not choose to believe it, but he would far rather be at home making fiddles than stuck on that exhausting musical merry-go-round. It was then that the first seeds of an idea came to him: a possible way to put an end to the failed agreement and solve the problem of Jenny. He went out into the kitchen, where he could think in peace and quiet.

4

About half a mile away, on the edge of the level plain at the bottom of the hill, Nancy McGrath called in on her elderly neighbour, Mikey Cullen. He always went across to see in the new year with Nancy and her family, and she had come over to collect him. But she found him in a poor state, huddled beside a feeble fire, shivering with cold.

Nancy put a blanket around his shoulders, stoked up the fire and made him a cup of tea. The old dog, Belle, followed at her heels until she realized that Mikey had either forgotten to feed her or was too ill to do it. That had never happened before.

'Are you all right, Mikey?' she said. 'You don't look too good.'

Mikey growled and pulled the blanket more tightly around his bony shoulders.

Nancy fed the dog. 'Will you come over to our house and toast the new year?'

'No, no,' said Mikey. He trembled, and the tea slopped on to the knee of his trousers. 'I'd hardly make it over there, I'd say.'

'I think you're sick, Mikey,' said Nancy. 'Shall I send for Dr Walsh?'

'No,' said Mikey. ''Tis way too late for Dr Walsh. You'd better send for Liddy.'

5

JJ answered his mobile and listened to what Nancy had to say. He had known Mikey Cullen all his life and was very fond of him. Since before JJ was born, Mikey had been a regular at the céilí dances that each successive generation of Liddys held every month in the converted barn beside the house. He had danced vigorously through his sixties, more sedately through his seventies and finally, at the age of eighty, he had hung up his boots. For another year or two he had continued to attend the céilís, sitting at the side of the dance floor and letting out a yelp of delight when the musicians made a particularly good key change. But over the last few months he had been absent, unable to make the walk across the fields and up the hill to the Liddy house. Any number of people had offered him lifts, but he wouldn't take them. He was happier at home, he said, beside his fire.

JJ missed his presence at the dances, and called over

to see him whenever he could find the time, and since Mikey couldn't come to the music, JJ took the music to him. It was not an act of charity. Mikey was always wonderful company. He was unusually tolerant for someone of his generation, and never had a bad word to say about anyone. He had been delighted to see the wave of immigrants that had started arriving in Ireland twenty or thirty years before, and had been the first person in the area to employ 'foreigners' to help him on the farm. He loved everyone, regardless of their failings, and there was no question now of JJ refusing his summons.

'Can I come?' said Donal when he heard where JJ was going.

JJ glanced at Aisling, who shrugged. 'I suppose so,' he said, looking at his watch again. 'We'll be back by midnight, assuming all's well.'

'Ring me if it isn't,' said Aisling.

Donal packed his old 'black dot' accordion into its box and JJ picked up his fiddle. Outside the rain had stopped and the cloud cover was breaking up. In patches of black silk sky, faint stars were showing. Somewhere, still hidden, the moon was almost full and the grey limestone crags above the farm looked as liquid as mercury in its filtered light.

It was a walk that JJ always enjoyed, but they took the car in case Mikey was seriously ill and needed to be taken anywhere. Donal sat in the passenger seat, silent and serious, clutching the box on his lap. He was a mystery to JJ; a calm, quiet child, almost invisible in a household full of large, colourful characters.

'Everything all right?' he asked him.

Donal looked across at him and smiled. 'I learned "The Cow That Ate the Blanket",' he said.

'Good man,' said JJ. 'We'll play that for Mikey tonight.'

Belle met them at the door. She had been beautiful in her younger days but now, owing to her habit of sleeping too close to the fire, her coat was singed all over and grimy with ashes.

Mikey struggled out of his chair.

'Sit down, sit down,' said JJ. 'How are you doing, Mikey?'

'Not so clever, JJ. But I'm not dead yet and I can still fetch a drink for a musicianer.'

'I won't take a drink, Mikey. I'm driving.'

'What harm?' said Mikey, pulling a bottle of whiskey from the dresser and reaching down glasses. 'You'll hardly meet the guards between here and your house.' He was unsteady on his feet and JJ shadowed him, ready to catch him if he fell. 'What'll the young lad drink?'

'I'm fine,' said Donal.

'Indeed you are fine,' said Mikey. He turned to JJ. 'Will he have a small drop? For the night that's in it?'

'He won't,' said JJ. 'He's only nine.'

But Mikey poured three large glasses anyway and then, leaning on the furniture, he made his way back to the fireside chair. As he lowered himself down into it he groaned.

'Oooh. All my joints are seized up, JJ.'

'You need a drop of oil, so,' said JJ.

'I do,' said Mikey. 'But I can't find out where to put it. Amazing they wouldn't tell you that, isn't it?'

JJ laughed. 'Do you not have the manual, Mikey?'

'Whatever about the manual, you have the cure there in your hand.' He pointed to the fiddle case and JJ and Donal began to unpack their instruments.

As they played, JJ wondered whether there wasn't some truth in what the old man had said. The music might not have freed up Mikey's joints but it, and no doubt the whiskey too, certainly lubricated his spirits. They played tunes that he knew and he called out their names and began keeping time; first with his fingers on the arm of his chair, then with his palms on his knees and, finally, with both feet on the ash-strewn hearth. Between the sets of tunes he reminisced about old times: the dances he had attended, the people he had met at them, the sweethearts he had never, in the end, married. By eleven o'clock, when he got up to refill his glass, he was a lot steadier than he had been and his cheeks had lost their unhealthy pallor. By eleven thirty, when JJ announced that it was time for them to go home, he looked ten years younger and he refused to let them leave without one more tune.

So Donal played 'The Cow That Ate the Blanket' and JJ quietly poured their untouched whiskey back into the bottle. There was no chance Mikey would notice. He was sitting up straight in his chair, slapping his knees and roaring, 'Go on, ya, boy, ya!' and 'Up Galway!' Donal played the tune through five times and finally wound up with a dramatic chord. Then he and JJ packed up their instruments and Mikey accompanied them, slowly but very steadily, to the front door and out into the yard.

The last of the cloud had drifted eastwards and the sky was clear. The moon was so bright that they could see each other's faces.

'You should lock your door, Mikey,' said JJ. 'You'd never know who might come wandering around these days.'

'Sure, if I lock the door how will I ever get out?' said Mikey mischievously. 'And, besides, who would I be afraid of? Amn't I the last of the High Kings?'

JJ had heard this before, many times. Not just from Mikey, either. There were people all over Ireland making the same claim. But it was new to Donal.

'Are you?' he said.

'I am,' said Mikey. 'And when I'm gone that will be the last of the Cullens. The last of the High Kings.' He swept an outstretched arm in a semicircle that might have encompassed the tiny yard, the whole of Moy and Funchin or the entire county of Galway. 'It all belonged to the Cullens at one time.'

The moonlight was even strong enough for JJ to see the face of his watch. It was eleven forty-five.

'Well, happy new year to you, Mikey,' he said, edging towards the car.

'The same to you,' said Mikey, 'and many happy returns.'

'Go in now, before you get cold,' said JJ.

'I will,' said Mikey, 'but come here. There's something I want you to do for me.'

'What's that?'

'I won't be seeing another new year.'

'Ah now—' JJ began, but Mikey cut him off.

'No, no. Hear me out. There's one last thing I want to do before I die.'

JJ was aware of the clock racing towards midnight. In another minute or two he was going to have to choose between offending Aisling and offending the old man. He wished Mikey had thought of saying all this at a better time.

'What is it you want to do?' he said.

Mikey pointed up past the Liddy house towards the top of the mountain. 'I want to go up there. I want to stand on top of the beacon one last time. Then I can rest in peace.'

JJ stared at him. There was no road to the top of the mountain. There wasn't even a path. Whichever direction you approached from, it was a long, steep climb, way beyond the capacities of a stiff old man like Mikey.

JJ laughed. 'There's only one way you'll get up there,' he said. 'And that's in a helicopter.'

Mikey nodded. 'That'll do rightly. Will you organize it, so?'

JJ had one last chance to avoid offending anybody. He hustled Donal towards the car.

'Leave it with me, Mikey,' he said. 'I'll see what I can do.'

6

Hazel came in, exhausted but extremely happy, at about three a.m. The minibus had dropped her at the end of the drive and she had walked up to the house in the moonlight. The boy she liked most in the world had smooched with her all night, and when she got back from Cork – if they ever got there – she was going out on a date with him. Everything seemed perfect.

She let herself into the house and closed the door quietly. The light from the upstairs landing spilled down into the hall and as she passed the sitting-room door she could see Jenny still sleeping on the sofa, and a couple of empty wine glasses beside the hearth. She was tempted to see if there was any wine left in the bottle but decided she'd probably had enough for one night, and went on up to bed.

She couldn't sleep, though. The house was silent but her mind was full of noise. She replayed the songs she had danced to with Desmond and tried to remember the things they had said, or shouted, to each other. She dreamed about what she would wear on their date, and how they would look together, and what everyone would say when they learned that Hazel and Desmond were an item.

At four thirty she was still awake, tired now of the circuit of imaginings but still charged with adrenalin. She got up to go to the bathroom and as she padded across the landing she heard, from downstairs, the soft creak of hinges and the snick of the Yale lock's tongue. She did a quick mental reckoning. The family were all in. There was only one thing that sound could mean. She hurtled down the stairs and out through the front door. If Jenny was running she would be too late already, and the trip to Cork would be delayed again.

But this time Jenny wasn't running. She was standing in the front yard, gazing up at the clear, white face of the moon. The cloudless skies had brought frost with them and Hazel winced as her bare feet met the icy flagstones. But Jenny didn't appear to notice the cold.

'The moon,' she said dreamily as Hazel came to stand at her side.

'The moon,' Hazel repeated. 'Still night-time, Jen. And we have to go to Cork tomorrow, remember?'

'I forgot,' said Jenny.

'Never mind,' said Hazel. She wasn't always so

patient with her wayward sister, but she was feeling adult and generous tonight. 'I think you'd better sleep with me in my bed now, in case you forget again.'

Jenny followed her back into the house and up to her bedroom.

'You hop into bed, Jen. I'll be back in a minute.'

This time Hazel made it to the bathroom, but she didn't make it back to bed. When she came out on to the landing she found her father sitting where she had been earlier, at the top of the stairs.

'Well caught, Hazey,' he said. 'Have you got a minute?'

'What, now?' said Hazel. She looked at her wrist, but her watch was on the bedside table.

'I know it's late,' said JJ, 'but this is important.'

Hazel sighed and sat down on the step beside him.

'Did you have a good night?'

'Brilliant,' said Hazel. She was tempted to tell him about the gorgeous Desmond but decided, for the moment at least, to keep it to herself.

'Good,' said JJ.

Hazel waited. JJ rubbed his palms together between his pyjama'd knees.

'Well?' said Hazel.

'Um,' he said. 'Well . . . I know this is going to sound a bit weird, but how would you feel about becoming a teenage mum?'

Hazel stared at him. In the pale glow of the landing light he looked old and tired. She could see dark rings beneath his eyes.

'Dad!' she said indignantly. In her wildest dreams she hadn't gone that far. 'I haven't even got a boyfriend yet! Well, at least—'

'No, no,' said JJ hurriedly. 'I don't mean really. I don't mean—' He ground to a halt and she could feel his embarrassment hanging in the cold air between them. He seemed unable to continue.

'Perhaps you'd better start at the beginning, Dad,' said Hazel.

JJ stood up and stretched. 'I think I'm going to let your mother do the driving tomorrow,' he said. 'I think I'm going to make a cup of tea now and tell you a very strange story.'

Down in the big farmhouse kitchen JJ told Hazel how, more than twenty-five years ago, he had gone to Tír na n'Óg, the land of eternal youth, and how he had met Aengus Óg, who had turned out to be his grandfather and was, therefore, her great-grandfather. He told her how he and Aengus had gone to meet the Dagda, who was the king of the fairies, and how they had found the time leak which had been destroying the two worlds.

The story, it seemed to Hazel, went from mad to

worse. There were times when she feared for her father's sanity and wondered whether she should slip off upstairs and wake her mother. The trouble was that some bits of it made sense. It explained why JJ was such an exceptional musician and why his playing was so distinctive. It explained why the fiddle he played sounded so much better than any other she had heard. So she stayed and listened, and when he finished telling her about that visit he told her some of the things that had happened since then, and why it was so important that she played her part in the plan he was hatching.

'Your mother can't have any more children,' he finished up. 'She had an operation after Aidan was born, and everybody knows that. Otherwise she could do it herself.'

'But I thought you said I didn't really have to have a baby?'

'You don't,' said JJ. 'But your mum couldn't even pretend to, you see? Everyone would know it wasn't hers.'

Hazel said nothing, and after a while JJ went on: 'Will you sleep on it, Hazey? Let me know tomorrow?'

Hazel thought it would probably be easier to sleep on a barbed-wire hammock than on the bizarre stories she had just been hearing. But she didn't want to say anything that would prolong the conversation.

'I suppose so,' she said, and escaped to the relative safety of her bed.

MAY

1

On a Friday afternoon in the middle of May a team of archaeologists walked up from the little car parking space at the entrance to the path which led to the ruin of St Coleman's church. They didn't follow the path, but turned to their left instead, crossed a few hundred metres of limestone pavement and began the ascent of Sliabh Carron from there. It wasn't the shortest way to the top but it was the easiest. This way there were no cliffs or craggy outcrops to contend with, and only two low walls to climb over.

There were five of them, two professionals and three students. They were heavily laden with tents and cooking gear and supplies of tinned and dried foods. The tools they would use for the excavation were still at their main base in Galway and they wouldn't be brought up until Monday, when the heavy work began. But they had brought their measuring equipment and their pegs and tape. The team leaders had been up to the huge barrow on several occasions, surveying it, analysing its construction and comparing it to other known monuments of a similar age. Today they would make their final measurements and mark out the precise area they had decided to excavate.

Professor Alice Kelly, the oldest member of the party and the official head of the team, stopped for a breather as the ascent grew steeper. The students were already way ahead of her, making light work of their big loads. She wondered how long their enthusiasm would last. There were several thousand tons of stones in that enormous cairn, and about a quarter of them would have to be carefully removed before they got an idea of what, if anything, was inside. From what she knew of the area and the age of the barrow, Alice suspected that the stones concealed a burial chamber, and probably one of considerable size. The prospect recharged her batteries almost instantaneously, and she resumed the climb.

It was an hour's walk from the road to the barrow. The climb took about half that time. The rest of the way, across the long, grassy back of the mountain, was almost level, but the going underfoot was treacherous, with thin soil and coarse grass covering much of the surface rock and concealing the grikes and holes in it. A twisted or broken ankle up there would be, if not a disaster, then at least a serious inconvenience. The students had been warned, and they slowed their pace accordingly, so by the time the barrow came into view the archaeologists were walking together in a group.

'There's someone there,' said Alice Kelly.

Her colleague, Professor David Connelly, was a keen birdwatcher. He lifted the binoculars that were hanging round his neck and looked through them.

'How extraordinary,' he said. 'It's a child. A little girl.'

2

Jenny, sitting on top of the hill of stones, watched the people approaching. She had seen plenty of back-packers – Kinvara was heaving with them in the summer – but she had never seen any up here before. It didn't surprise her that they would want to come and see what was on top of the mountain, but she couldn't understand why they would want to bring so much stuff with them.

Stuff, and the attachment that people had to it, was a source of constant bewilderment to Jenny. Hazel's room was crammed full of things but she was forever complaining that she hadn't enough money for clothes and CDs and that she couldn't afford to buy the latest thing for sticking her earphones into. Donal had loads of stuff, too. He had mountains of toys he never played with and books he had already read and DVDs he had already seen, and his drawers were overflowing with clothes he had grown out of. Jenny liked her room empty and clear. Most of the stuff that was in it she didn't want, and she was always putting things in the bin. Hairbrushes and go-go bands and clothes she didn't like and never wore. Shoes. It was a waste of time, really. Aisling or JJ always took them back out and cluttered up her room with them again.

But when she came up here, as she did nearly every day now, she brought nothing with her at all. If it was really cold and windy she sometimes wore a jacket, but that was all. What could those people possibly have in their rucksacks? It was beyond Jenny's capacity to imagine.

Alice Kelly dropped her gear at the foot of the barrow and, feeling delightfully weightless, walked up the side of it to where the little girl was sitting. Despite a fresh breeze, the child wore only a light cotton frock, and her feet were bare. She looked like something from another century.

'Hello,' said Alice, trying her best to sound friendly. 'What are you doing up here?'

'I'm talking to the ghost,' said Jenny.

Alice felt a chill run through her. She had always found this mountain a bit creepy, and today it had been worse than ever. A huge white goat had appeared when they got to the top, and it had followed them, keeping its distance, all the way. It was still there now, a few hundred metres away, still watching every move they made. And now here was this child, who was so thin and pale she might almost be a ghost herself.

Alice glanced back down the slope of the barrow but the others, as though they were a bit apprehensive themselves, were showing no inclination to follow her.

'Is there a ghost?' she said. 'I can't see it.'

'There's only one way to see a ghost,' said the child. 'You'll never see it if you're looking at it. You only see them when you're looking the other way, and only out of the corner of your eye.'

'Really?' said Alice.

'I had to figure that out for myself,' said Jenny, a little proudly.

With an effort, Alice remembered where she was and what she was doing there. She was, she decided, taking all this far too seriously.

'That's clever of you,' she said, assuming a patronizing tone that was as familiar to Jenny as it is to most children. 'And what's your name?'

'Jenny.'

'Jenny who?'

'Jenny Liddy,' said Jenny. 'Why have you brought all that stuff with you?'

'Because we're archaeologists,' said Alice. 'Do you know what an archaeologist is?'

'Yes,' said Jenny.

'Good. Well, I'm Professor Kelly and this is my research team. We're going to excavate this barrow. Do you know what excavate means?'

'Yes,' said Jenny. 'But I don't think he'll let you do that.'

'Who won't?' said Alice.

'The ghost,' said Jenny.

Alice Kelly took a deep breath. 'We have a lot of work to do,' she said. 'I'd better be making a start.' She turned to go back down the hill of stones, then stopped and turned back.

'Shouldn't you be in school?' she said.

'Yes,' said Jenny.

3

The archaeologists had brought two large tents with them. One was for use as a work station, for cleaning any artefacts they might find, and for drawing and photographing them, and for writing up progress notes. The other was a mess tent, where the team could take a break and make tea and meals. Everyone there knew that they were in for the long haul. This project was going to be not so much a dig as a rock haulage camp for at least the first few weeks. It would be tedious, back-breaking work and it would have to be done slowly and carefully, with each stone examined and numbered, so that it could be put back in pretty much the same place when the job was finished. The sheer size of the barrow and its isolated location were the main reasons it had never been excavated before.

It was soon clear to the team that nothing up there on that mountain was going to be easy. The occasional sheltered hollow had, over the years, accumulated enough soil to drive a tent peg into, but there were none of these in the vicinity of the beacon. Everywhere the team looked they found the same thing. Limestone rock lying on or just beneath the surface. They agreed on a campsite eventually, but there was no way their tent pegs would hold in the thin soil. There were stones on the barrow that would have anchored the flapping guy ropes, but the team leaders wouldn't allow them to be used. Instead the students were sent off to search the bleak landscape for stray rocks, and to cart them back across the treacherous ground. The breeze strengthened as they unpacked the tents, and it snatched at the light fabric, making it next to impossible to construct the frames. In the end two of the students were consigned to lie inside the tent shells and hold them down, while the others struggled to get them secured. It took most of the morning for them to get the tents up, and when they finally succeeded and had gathered inside the smaller one to get something to eat, they all agreed that it would have been a lot easier if they hadn't been under such close scrutiny.

'There's something weird about that child,' said David Connelly. 'How come she isn't freezing up there?'

'I don't mind the child so much,' said one of the

students. 'It's that frigging white goat that puts the wind up me.'

When they came out again after their lunch, both the observers were still there, Jenny up on the top of the beacon and the goat, just visible, on the flat horizon of the hilltop. They continued to watch as the archaeologists set up their tripods and tapes and measured the barrow from every conceivable angle, and set down coloured markers, and moved them, and set them down again. They watched as the team finalized their measurements and set up the boundaries of the excavation area with wooden sticks and orange twine. They watched as the five of them finished up with that and stood together, admiring their day's work.

Jenny waited eagerly to see what would happen next. Nothing that the archaeologists had done so far had bothered the ghost. Over the thirty centuries that he had been there, thousands of people had visited the heap of stones. Some had sat up there and meditated upon the view. Some had come with friends and families, and brought food with them to share. Some had brought a small stone to add to the pile, and others had taken one away with them as a souvenir. None of these things had caused the ghost the slightest concern. He loved people, he told her. The human race was the pinnacle of perfection, the lord of all beasts, equal in beauty and valour to the gods. The thing that had sustained him throughout the thousands of years that he had guarded the beacon was the knowledge that he, and he alone, was keeping the world safe for humankind. That made him proud, even though he knew he had been forgotten. No one, he told Jenny, had ever come to talk with him the way she did. Since the time he died, he had never had a friend.

Jenny had never had a friend before, either. There was the púca of course, but he was more like a teacher or a kindly old uncle than a friend. And anyway, she wasn't sure he really counted, because he was a goat. A sort of a goat, anyway. Sometimes he changed and looked more like a goaty kind of man, but mostly he looked like a goat.

She wasn't really sure that the ghost counted, either. He couldn't come to dinner and for sleepovers like Hazel's friends did. He couldn't practise hurling or play computer games like Donal's friends did. He couldn't even go with her on her explorations of the mountains and the woods, because ghosts, he had told her, were anchored to the place where they died. But he was, Jenny decided, a kind of friend all the same. She liked coming up here to visit him and to look out over the plain towards the shining sea, and to hear about his life, and about how it had felt to die.

The archaeologists stood around for a while, looking at the barrow, and at Jenny, and at the sky. Then
they went back into the smaller tent and, after a while,
one of the young people came out and brought Jenny
a cup of hot, sweet coffee and a little pile of chocolate
biscuits.

'I'm Maureen,' she said, sitting down beside her.
'What's your name?'

'Jenny.'

'Aren't you cold, Jenny?'

'No,' said Jenny, accepting the coffee but not the
biscuits. 'Why do you want to excavate the beacon?'

'The beacon?' said Maureen. 'Is that what you call
it?'

'What do you think you'll find inside it?' said Jenny,
unwilling to allow the subject to be changed.

'Well,' said Maureen, 'we don't want to try and
predict, but we're hoping there will be an ancient
burial chamber in there, and maybe some remains of
whoever was buried in it.'

'There won't be any,' said Jenny.

'We'll have to wait and see, won't we?' said Maureen.
She waited, and when Jenny said nothing more, she
went on: 'Won't your parents be wondering where you
are?'

Jenny considered this carefully. Maureen had
touched upon another of those things which, like the

desire for stuff, Jenny found impossible to understand. If what people said was true most of them seemed to have the ability to know, or at least to guess, what other people were thinking and feeling. But Jenny couldn't do it. She couldn't even remember to try to do it, even though she was constantly being told off for having no consideration. According to her family she was always hurting someone's feelings or making their lives miserable. The problem was that she couldn't really see how a feeling could be hurt, and although she had seen other people being miserable she hadn't ever been miserable herself and she didn't understand how someone else could make her feel that way. If she didn't like what was happening she found a way of changing it. Being miserable seemed to her like a waste of valuable time.

So, would her parents be wondering where she was? 'They might be.'

'Do you often come up here?' said Maureen.

'Yes,' said Jenny. 'What are you going to do next?'

'Nothing else today,' said Maureen. 'We're just waiting on a delivery.'

4

Donal walked down the drive and crossed the New Line; the road that ran along the edge of the mountain range between New Quay and the Ennis-to-Galway road. He climbed over the wall at the other side and went through the fields to Mikey Cullen's house. Two or three times a week now he put the accordion into the new backpack that JJ had bought him, and made the short trip over to see Mikey. To begin with he had only walked when there was no possibility of cadging a lift, but lately, now that the weather was milder and the evenings were longer, he had come to enjoy the quiet time by himself. He noticed that the light, and the feel of the air and the way it smelled, were different every day. And he liked talking to Peter Hayes's cattle, which were down from the mountain now and grazing Mikey's home meadows. They seemed to like talking to him as well, and always came bunching around him when he appeared.

Donal was still too young to play at the classes and céilís that were held at his house at weekends, but he was not too young to enjoy the pleasure that his music could bring to other people. He liked playing at home with his parents and Hazel, but he was always aware that they were accommodating him, and that they played with more speed and energy when he wasn't joining in and slowing them down. But playing for Mikey was something entirely different. He was able to settle into his own steady rhythm, and the old man's enthusiasm and encouragement lifted his spirits and made him feel like a real musician.

Early in the new year JJ had enlisted the help of Eoin O'Neill, a box player who was also a plumber, and they had, despite Mikey's protestations, fitted a simple central heating system in the old house. It came on automatically every morning and evening, and although Mikey still complained about it there was no denying that he was in better health on account of it. He was still a bit stiff and nothing was going to make him any younger, but the threat of hypothermia no longer lurked in damp corners and his persistent, wheezy cough had completely cleared up.

Donal knocked at the door and went in. There was no sign of Mikey. Donal called, then checked in the kitchen and the bathroom and bedroom. He put the box down on the chair beside the fireplace and went back out into the yard. Belle appeared from behind the house and came to greet him. He patted her shoulder, noticing that her fine ginger coat was growing back. She too had benefited from the central heating.

'Where's Mikey?' Donal asked her.

She wagged her tail and whined. Donal walked in the direction from which she had come, towards the haggard where Mikey's vegetable patch had been when he was still strong enough to manage it. Now it was just nettles and brambles, but there was a well-worn path through the middle of them, leading to the old fort which lay between the house and the meadows beyond.

Donal had explored it before. It wasn't much of a fort. There were a few metres of tumbledown stone wall on one side and some lumpy patches of ground in the middle that might once have been the sites of dwellings, but the rest of the area was choked with twisted old ash and blackthorn trees. That was where Mikey was now, hidden by the foliage. Donal could hear him talking to someone.

'You know I would if I could,' he was saying. 'But look at the state of me. I can barely get out of bed in the mornings, let alone—'

'Mikey?' Donal called.

There was a rustle of bushes and Mikey came out,

bending with difficulty beneath some low branches.

'Donal Liddy,' he said cheerfully. 'Come down from the mountainside to play me a tune.'

'Who were you talking to?' said Donal.

Mikey looked at him carefully for a moment, then said: 'Ach, no one. Myself, that's who I was talking to.'

Belle, Donal noticed, had a bad habit of walking right in front of Mikey and obstructing his progress. It was for all the right reasons – she was watching him carefully and waiting for him – but it could be dangerous as well. If Mikey wasn't looking he could easily trip over her. She preceded them now as they went into the house, and while Mikey made tea in the kitchen Donal swept the hearth, took out the ashes and brought in a basket of turf. He added a few sods of it to the bright embers, still burning from the night before, then sat down in the high-backed chair and unpacked the accordion.

'You don't really need this fire any more,' he said when Mikey came in with the tea. 'Now that you've got the central heating.'

'What would I look at in the evenings?' said Mikey. 'You can't watch central heating. Besides, there has been a fire burning in this spot for thousands of years. That same fire there burned in front of the first of the

High Kings and it never went out since, not once. When I'm dead, then we can let it out.'

They drank their tea, then Donal played tunes and Mikey yipped and roared and tapped the spotless hearth with his booted feet. Donal showed him the new tunes he had learned and Mikey requested old favourites, and before either of them knew it an hour had passed and the new sods of turf were producing a rich, red heat. The little session was just reaching a natural conclusion when Mikey heard the helicopter.

'Is that my one?' he asked, making for the front door with surprising speed. 'Did JJ send it for me?'

'I don't think so,' said Donal, putting down the box and following him out into the yard.

Together they scanned the skies. They couldn't see the helicopter but they could still hear it. It sounded as if it was hovering somewhere over the mountain, but too low for them to see it from where they stood. Mikey leaned against the wall and they waited for it to appear. It didn't. The noise of its engines stayed constant, just maddeningly out of sight.

'What's it doing up there?' said Mikey.

'I don't know,' said Donal.

They waited and waited, but still the machine didn't appear.

'Is it a helicopter?' said Mikey.

'Oh it is,' said Donal. 'It's definitely a chopper.'

'A chopper,' Mikey repeated, grinning at the word. 'It sounds like it's coming from the beacon. What would it be doing at the beacon?'

Eventually, when they had been waiting for about ten minutes, the engine sound changed and the helicopter passed above them, heading back towards Kinvara and Galway Bay.

'Well, blast it anyway,' said Mikey, detaching himself from the wall. 'When is my one going to come?'

5

The archaeologists had brought enough water with them up the mountain to last them for the day, but when the work began in earnest the following week they were going to need far more of it than they could carry. Their budget didn't come anywhere close to providing helicopter assistance, but Alice Kelly had persuaded the air-sea rescue to help them out. They had agreed on the grounds that it would provide a good training exercise, and it had been their chopper that Mikey and Donal had heard above the mountain.

From where Jenny was sitting on the top of the beacon the roar of the engine and the clatter of the rotor blades was deafening. She had seen helicopters before on her visits up there, and once a pilot had passed close enough to wave at her. But this was quite different. That thing up there was a huge, bellowing, violent creature and she didn't like it one little bit.

The drop went like clockwork. The rescue crew

lowered the fifty-gallon drums, two at a time, on the winch line. David Connelly guided them to the ground and unclipped them, and the students lugged them away and stacked them between the two tents. There were twelve containers in all; six hundred gallons of fresh water. When the last one was safely landed and the winch line freed, Alice Kelly waved to the pilot. The door of the chopper closed and it drifted sideways across the mountain top, set its nose towards the sea and powered away over the plain.

In the resounding silence left in its wake, Alice thought she caught a glimpse, out of the corner of her eye, of a slim figure standing on top of the barrow. But when she turned to look, there was no one there.

'Where did the little girl go?' she asked the others. But no one had seen Jenny, or the big white goat for that matter, as they slipped away and headed down the side of the mountain.

6

JJ finished shaping the new bridge he was making for Sean Pearce's fiddle and glanced at the clock. It was nearly five and it was his turn to make the dinner. He set the bridge aside. Tomorrow, or perhaps later tonight, he would string up the fiddle and try it out. He might have to make some adjustments to the position of the soundpost, but essentially the job was finished, which meant that he would have one less disgruntled customer on his back. There were still quite a few to go, though. He looked at the rack of instruments on the wall then looked away again before he could be tempted to start counting them. Some of those fiddles had been hanging there, awaiting his attention, for more than a year.

The problem, as he saw it, was that he was trying to live two lives. Three, if you counted being a father and housekeeper as well. He would have been happy to give up the touring, or most of it, but he couldn't make a decent living from the fiddle business unless he could sell some of his own, handmade instruments. And he couldn't make the kind of instruments he wanted to make until he got the wood from the chiming maple that Aengus had promised him.

He sighed and began to put away his tools. He should have known better than to trust Aengus Óg. He should have agreed to nothing without seeing the wood first. He was sure that he would get it soon – the wheels were already in motion – but he had already waited far too long, and as he thought about it he found it hard to believe that he had let it happen. If he had got the wood when he should have done he would be making fiddles from it by now. As it was, even if he got it tomorrow he would have to wait another eight or ten years before it was dried and cured and ready to be used.

He glanced around the workshop. It looked as if a tornado had recently passed through it. Every level surface was cluttered with old cases, half-made or half-mended instruments, bows, tools, fittings and strings, wood-shavings, dust. At Newark, where he had learned his trade, the teachers drummed it into the students again and again. *Keep the workbench tidy*. JJ was afraid that his workshop was a reflection of his personality. If it was, then it showed him to be careless and sloppy, and unable to attend to the basics.

He looked at the clock again. He had time to finish off that fiddle and still get the dinner on. But instead of going back to work he gazed out of the window. The workshop was at the back of the house and gave him a view out across the farm and the steep slope of the mountainside beyond. Far over to the right he could see a small band of wild goats, browsing their way across the edge of the crag. A few hundred metres to their left, completely separate from them, was another goat, a single white one, making its way down the hillside. It was the one he had seen when he went looking for Jenny on New Year's Eve, and he noticed now that she was there as well, trotting along close behind it. Even as he watched, the goat stopped and waited for Jenny to catch up with it.

JJ stared at them, deeply troubled. He knew a lot about goats. His parents had run a herd of them on this farm when he was growing up. The room where he sat now had originally been built on to the house as a place for making cheese. When JJ first married, he and Aisling had intended to keep the business going, but then JJ had gone to college, and after that his musical career had taken off, and he was away too much of the time. Aisling couldn't manage the farm and the family on her own and eventually, reluctantly, they had sold the goats. JJ had missed them more than he had expected. They had been a part of his life and even when he saw wild ones on the mountain he felt that he knew them inside out.

But not this white one. He had never seen any goat, wild or domesticated, behave like this. As he watched, it folded its knees and lay down on its belly on a patch of grass. Jenny sat cross-legged beside it. They were much too far away for JJ to see any details, but it was clear that Jenny and the goat were extremely comfortable with each other. They looked like a couple of friends sitting down to have a chat. And JJ was very afraid that was exactly what they were doing.

7

Hazel burst in through the front door and slung her school bag the full length of the hall.

'Freedom!' she yelled, at no one in particular.

Her mother was in the sitting room reading a homeopathy text. There was evidence that she had been showing Aidan how to make potato prints with poster paints, but at the moment he was busy hacking the spud halves into pieces with a pair of scissors.

'What's for dinner?' said Hazel.

Aisling looked up from her book and shrugged. 'Your dad's cooking.'

'Oh, no,' said Hazel. 'That means we won't be eating until ten o'clock.'

'Oh, no,' said Aidan, stabbing one of the colourful prints through the dead centre with surprising accuracy.

'Can I make beans on toast?' said Hazel.

Aisling put the book down and stood up. 'Yeah.

And make some for his nibs as well or we'll never see the back of him.'

Aisling set about separating Aidan from the scissors and Hazel went into the kitchen. She found JJ in there, peering into cupboards.

'What are we having for dinner?' she asked him.

'Erm—' he said.

'You forgot to go shopping, didn't you?' she said.

'I didn't forget exactly,' said JJ. 'I just—'

'Forgot,' said Hazel. 'You'd better go now. I'll hold the fort here.'

In the yard, on his way to get the car, JJ met Donal returning from Mikey's with the accordion.

'Where are you going?' Donal asked.

'Just to the village,' said JJ. 'Back in ten minutes.'

Donal knew it took ten minutes to get to the village and another ten minutes to get back. Presumably there was some reason to be going there, which would also take some number of minutes as well. His father had never been any good where time was concerned. But Donal knew a great deal about it. He knew, for instance, how rare it was for him to get some of it alone with his father, and he knew how much of it he would need to pick a small bone with him. That was why, without another word, he opened the passenger door of the car and got in.

Hazel loved having the old kitchen to herself. She decided she needed a cup of tea before she did anything else, and while she waited for the kettle to boil she sat in the elderly horsehair armchair beside the range and enjoyed the solitary moment.

She had been through a rough time. The affair with Desmond had come to an early conclusion, and it had knocked her confidence badly. Although her friends had been sympathetic there was a strong underlying current along the lines of 'I told you so' running through their condolences. Desmond was one of those guys. 'A bit of a lad' was what some people called him, though Hazel used other, less diplomatic terms. He was always stringing girls along, and Hazel had been embarrassed to discover that, if all Desmond's ex-girlfriends had been gathered together in one place, they could have filled a double-decker bus.

She hadn't told her parents, but it was during her depression following the break-up that she had agreed to play her part in JJ's plan. She didn't want to go clubbing and see Desmond chatting up her successors, and although she didn't tell her friends the reason, she had a ready-made excuse for going around wearing bulky jumpers and a long face. And when she came back from Dublin, having apparently had a baby, people could draw their own conclusions about who its father was. That would be up to them. She was saying nothing, not now and not ever.

She wasn't exactly happy about it, but she could see that this wild scheme of her father's had its advantages. He was treating her like royalty for one thing, and she was looking forward to going to Dublin and being spoiled by her grandparents, Helen and Ciaran. Best of all, she was getting an extra fortnight off school. Term didn't finish for her class until the end of May but her mother had written a letter, deliberately ambiguous, saying that Hazel needed the last two weeks off 'for health reasons'. She was between her Junior and Leaving Cert years, so nothing was to be lost by missing a few end-of-term lessons.

The kettle boiled and she got up to make the tea. A brief cloud of anxiety crossed her mind when she thought about what she would have to face when she came home again in August, but she decided to ignore it. Tomorrow she would be on the Dublin train, and she just couldn't wait.

'Dad?' said Donal to JJ as they drove towards the village.

'Hmm?' said JJ.

Donal waited, watching the passing hedgerows, which were flush with the shining green of early summer. It was a deliberate ploy, this waiting. He knew how good adults were at pretending to listen when, in fact, their minds were working away furiously at something entirely different.

'What is it?' JJ said at last.

Confident that he now had his father's attention, Donal said: 'When are you going to get the chopper for Mikey?'

'When am I what?'

'To take him up the mountain. You said you would.'

JJ slowed to negotiate an oncoming tractor on the narrow road. 'No I didn't,' he said.

'You did. He said he wanted to go up to the beacon and you said the only way he'd get up there was in a chopper, and you said—'

'I was only messing, Donal,' said JJ. 'Where would I get a chopper?'

Donal looked out of the window again. They were nearer the village now and there were new houses every few metres, some of them only half built. There was nowhere comfortable for him to rest his eyes.

'Well,' he said at last. 'You'd better tell him you were only messing. He thinks you meant it.'

JJ slowed again, for a van this time. He wondered how his family had come to be so bizarre. He had a daughter at home pretending to be pregnant, a son in his car expecting him to produce a helicopter and, weirdest of all . . . He tried to steer his mind away from Jenny and the thing, possibly a goat but probably not, that she appeared to have befriended. It took his mind cleanly away from Mikey and the chopper.

Donal saw his father's face glaze over and knew he had lost his attention. He sighed and turned away again. He was on his own in this. There was no help to be had from JJ.

8

When JJ got home Jenny was in the armchair in the kitchen and, as far as he could see, she hadn't brought her big white friend with her. He would have liked to ask her about it, but she was engaged in an occupation that was of such value to himself and the rest of the family that he was reluctant to divert her attention. She was reading a book to Aidan.

The effect that Jenny had upon the toddler was remarkable. Unless he was exhausted or hurt he would never sit on anybody's knee except Jenny's. He was always far too busy storming around the place and looking for things that weren't broken yet. His parents were allowed to read him a story at bed time, but at any other time of day that privilege was reserved for Jenny. It always amazed JJ to see the transformation that came over him at those times. His square-shouldered posture and his firmly set jaw would relax as he settled back against Jenny's skinny frame, and a kind of blissful calm would come over his features.

JJ moved carefully around the kitchen, making himself as small and as quiet as possible. He cleared away the dirty plates and washed the saucepan that the beans had been in. Then he started to chop onions. Jenny read on. JJ risked a glance in her direction and saw that she was still pointing to each word as she read it. She had a reading age of about seven, the teacher said, but to JJ and Aisling it had been a cause for celebration, because it had looked for years as though Jenny would never learn to read at all. She wasn't stupid by any means, and she wasn't lazy. She simply wasn't interested. School was an ordeal for her; a torment to be endured on those days when she didn't succeed in escaping to the hills. It was a bit of an ordeal for her teachers as well, who found it practically impossible to get her to concentrate on anything, and who couldn't let her out of their sight for a moment in case she slipped out and made her way home. From her third year in school she had been under the supervision of a remedial teacher, but it had been a long time before Jenny had made any progress. It was only recently that she had begun to enjoy reading, and she particularly enjoyed reading to Aidan.

JJ fried onions and added minced beef. Jenny came to the end of the book and Aidan said: 'Again! Again!'

They were reading a picture book called *I Am I*,

which Aidan insisted on taking out of the library time after time. It was about two boys engaged in a struggle for power. Jenny loved the pictures, especially the one of the dragon, but she didn't really understand what it was about. It was more of that feeling stuff, about wanting and fighting. She suspected, though she couldn't be sure, that little Aidan already understood it far better than she did.

9

It was Jenny's turn to wash up, but that didn't really mean anything. It wasn't that she objected to taking her turn. She didn't. The problem was that when Jenny tried to wash up, or to do anything else that required a certain amount of application, it somehow never got finished. No matter how hard she tried to concentrate, her mind just wouldn't stay where she put it. There had been too many occasions when the others on the clear-up squad had stood waiting, tea-towels in hand, while Jenny gazed absently out of the window or stared in wonderment at the detergent bubbles. It was far quicker and far less stressful for everyone if someone else took over.

It had, in the past, caused serious friction. On one occasion, when Hazel was fourteen, she had threatened to leave home on account of the unfairness of it all. But by now everyone had got used to it and there were few hard feelings. Jenny was Jenny, and nothing anyone could do was going to change her.

JJ had cooked so he was relieved of clean-up duties. He left Aisling in charge and followed Jenny, as casually as he could, into the sitting room. She was underneath the TV, taking the plug out of the wall. JJ sat on the sofa and picked up Aisling's in-comprehensible textbook, and wondered how to bring up the subject of goats in a casual way. 'Who was that goat I saw you with today?' didn't quite fit the bill. He tried a different tack.

'I think you forgot about school again today, didn't you?'

'I think I did,' said Jenny.

'Where did you go?'

Jenny pointed up in the direction of the mountain.

'And did you meet anyone up there?' said JJ.

'I did,' said Jenny.

'Who?' said JJ.

Jenny thought about this for a moment or two. She had tried to tell JJ about the ghost once before, but he had told her there was no such thing as ghosts. She had told Hazel about the púca, and Hazel had said something along the same lines but with added insults.

'I met some archaeologists,' she said.

JJ sat up. 'Archaeologists?'

'Five of them,' said Jenny.

JJ remembered hearing something about a dig, but it had been a while ago and he had forgotten all about it.

'They are going to try and excavate the beacon,' Jenny went on, 'but they won't be able to.'

'Why not?'

Jenny thought hard. 'Because somebody there is no such thing as won't let them.'

JJ frowned at her. 'Somebody there's no such thing as?'

'And anyway,' said Jenny, eager to move on, 'they would only be disappointed. They think there's an old tomb or something in there, but there isn't.'

'How do you know?'

Jenny was getting tired of the conversation. She began to fidget and glance towards the hallway, longing for the refuge of her bedroom. 'The ghost told me,' she said.

'I see,' said JJ. He was beginning to realize that there was no point in asking Jenny about the goat or anything else for that matter. She inhabited a different world from the rest of them and, as far as he could make out, it was imagined afresh every day. Besides, she was edging towards the door.

'So what is under the beacon, then?'

Jenny had to think about that question as well. The ghost could hear and understand when she spoke to him but he had no voice so he couldn't speak back to her in words. He spoke to her in thoughts instead, and sometimes there were Irish words in among the thoughts that she understood, and more often there weren't. But there were usually images. If she tried to look at them too hard they vanished, just as the ghost himself did if you looked straight at him. But if she let the images rest gently on the peripheries of her mind and waited, they usually became clear sooner or later. It was a skill that had taken her some considerable time to acquire, and Jenny found herself wondering why there were no exams in school on talking to ghosts.

'Jenny?' said JJ.

'Hmm?'

'What is under the beacon?'

She could see it quite clearly in her mind's eye, but it had come from the ghost with no word attached. She made a stab at it.

'A chopper,' she said, and while JJ stared at her in stunned amazement, she fled.

10

'It's not going to work,' said Aisling to JJ as she got into bed beside him that night.

'It has to,' said JJ. 'I can't see any other option.' He moved over to give her more space. 'Besides, she's getting madder and madder. Do you know what she told me this evening?'

'What?'

'She said there's a helicopter under the beacon.'

'Oh, dear,' said Aisling. She tried to keep a straight face, but JJ knew what was coming. Aisling's emotions were always close to the surface. She got angry easily, she cried easily, but most of all she laughed easily, and this was the thing that JJ loved best about her. She burst into a fit of the giggles and JJ couldn't stop himself from joining in. It was a long time before they were finished with laughing, and it was another long time before Aisling remembered what it was they had been talking about. When she did, her face became serious again.

'It just seems there are so many things that can go wrong,' she said. 'What if they don't believe that it's Hazel's baby? What if they examine her?'

'Why should they?' said JJ. 'There's nothing criminal about having a baby. Why wouldn't they believe her?'

Aisling sighed and turned to face him. 'Maybe,' she said. 'But what about Jenny? They'll think we murdered her or something.'

'Of course they won't!'

But JJ was anxious about that part as well. He wondered whether the Gardai kept records and, if so, for how long. His family had a bit of a history where unexplained disappearances were concerned. There was the priest, Father Doherty, who some people still believed had been murdered by JJ's great-grandfather following a row about a flute. His remains had finally come to light in the souterrain at the time of JJ's own mysterious disappearance. He knew where he had been for that missing month, of course, and he had let Aisling and his parents and Hazel into the secret. But the authorities never did solve the mystery, and if there was another Liddy disappearance they might start raking over old coals and asking awkward questions.

He put an arm around Aisling. 'We can call it all off if you want to,' he said. 'It's still not too late.'

'But if we call it off you won't get your wood.'

'I can live without the wood.'

'But I'll be stuck at home with Jenny for another five or six years, and you'll be off gallivanting around the world with your fiddle.'

There was another alternative, but JJ was reluctant to suggest it. He could stay at home and work on the fiddles without the chiming maple from Tír na n'Óg. It would be a compromise, and he might not make much of an income, but Aisling could go back to work and between them they would make a living. It was the principle of the thing that flushed JJ's cheeks with anger. Aengus had promised him the wood and hadn't delivered. Why should JJ be the one to compromise?

'It'll work,' he said to Aisling. 'It has to.'

They lay in silence, and after a while JJ became aware that Aisling was struggling with tears. He rubbed her shoulder.

'What's up?'

Aisling shook her head. 'It's Jenny,' she spluttered, through her tears. 'She's the weirdest child in the world and she drives me up the wall, but that doesn't mean I won't miss her when she's gone.'

11

The púca never went anywhere near the beacon, but Jenny could usually see him from the top of it, standing on the horizon with his back to the wind, or browsing among the rocks. Sometimes the wild goats came along, on their way from one part of the mountain to another, and occasionally the white goat joined them for a while, though rarely for long.

Jenny had been waiting for the archaeologists since soon after dawn. Their tents were still there and so were the twelve white canisters that hadn't been there yesterday when she left, but there weren't any people. Jenny had no watch so she couldn't be sure what time it was, but she had a suspicion that they wouldn't be coming today. She couldn't be sure, but she had an idea it might be Saturday.

Someone else came up there to join her, though. JJ and Donal. It was around midday when they arrived, judging by the sun.

'We brought a picnic,' said Donal, gesturing towards the knapsack on JJ's back. He was cheerful now, but he hadn't been when they set out. JJ had prised him away from the computer with a combination of bribes and threats. He couldn't understand why the children, with the obvious exception of Jenny, didn't get outside more. He hated seeing them transfixed in front of TV and computer screens. He wanted them to share his pleasure in scrambling around on the wild, stony mountainside.

'No sign of the archaeologists, then?' he said to Jenny. She shook her head.

'Any ghosts?'

'Just the one,' said Jenny. 'The usual one.'

JJ nodded. 'And what about púcas? Any púcas?'

Jenny wasn't sure how to deal with that question. It sounded as though JJ was making fun of her. She scanned the horizon but, as it happened, the white goat was nowhere to be seen.

'No,' she said. 'Not that I can see.'

Donal was unpacking the knapsack. 'It's cool up here,' he said. 'Can I come up here instead of going to school like Jenny does?'

'No you can't,' said JJ. 'No way.'

'Why not?' said Donal. 'It's not fair. She never—' He broke off and glanced around sharply, his eyes wide with surprise.

'What is it?' said JJ.

'Nothing,' said Donal. 'I just thought I saw—'

'What?'

'Nothing,' said Donal again. He carried on unpacking the picnic and JJ watched him uneasily, but if he saw anything else he didn't mention it.

'Did you know we were sitting on a helicopter?' JJ asked him.

'A helicopter?'

'According to Jenny, anyway.'

'I didn't say that!' said Jenny indignantly.

'What did you say, then?'

'I said a chopper. For chopping.'

'Oh, that kind of chopper,' said JJ. 'I see. Like an axe? For chopping wood?'

'Yes, it's like a little axe,' said Jenny, 'but it's not for chopping wood.'

'For chopping what, then?' said JJ.

Jenny shrugged. 'People, I think.'

Donal handed round sandwiches and for a while the three of them munched in silence. Jenny had no objection to their company but she didn't like JJ's mood and the way he seemed to be teasing her. She wasn't very good at judging what other people were thinking, but she could tell there was a reason for JJ's questions and that something was making him uncomfortable. She hoped that he had finished now, and that he would want to talk about something else, but after a while he came back to the ghost again, in the same mock-humorous tone.

'So why is the people-chopper so important? Why doesn't the ghost want the archaeologists to find it?'

That was a hard question. Jenny had asked it before, but the ghost's answers had been very confusing. They involved people cutting down forests, and gruesome battles with enormous powerful beasts that Jenny had no name for, and families being driven from their homes.

'I don't know,' she said to JJ. 'I don't understand it myself.'

'Oh, well,' said JJ. 'I suppose we'll find out some day.' He threw the slops of his tea down between the stones and began to pack away the remains of the picnic. 'I'm going to tramp along the top and go home by way of Coleman's church. Anyone want to come?'

Jenny was game but Donal shook his head. 'I'm going to play some tunes for Mikey,' he said. 'Why don't you come with me, Jenny? You could bring your whistle.'

Jenny considered this. On the whole she favoured the tramping option, but she was wary of JJ's mood and she didn't want to answer any more questions.

'OK,' she said to Donal. 'We can look for my shoes on the way home.'

12

JJ strode out across the top of Sliabh Carron. It was an eerie place, strewn with untidy reminders of past generations. Perhaps a historian or one of those archaeologists could have made sense of the broken stone structures that he passed every few minutes, but JJ couldn't. He had no way of knowing whether this heap of rocks or those broken walls were two hundred or two thousand years old, but there was one thing he could tell. The people who had built them had done their thinking in circles and not in squares.

He breathed deeply. The air was cool and sweet and he could feel the colour returning to his cheeks. Like the children, he spent far too much of his time indoors. It was a kind of half-life, he decided. Only out here on the broad, scraggy pelt of the planet did he feel fully alive.

It was common enough around those parts for a tired old cloud to lose its way and blunder into the top

93

of the mountains. JJ saw one coming, and minutes later he was inside it, walking through a fine, sparkly drizzle, moving within a white dome of mist. The damp formed droplets on his clothes and his hair. It was his favourite kind of weather. It gave him energy. He could have walked for ever through this soft, fresh day. This, he told himself, was what being alive was all about. Maybe giving up the goats had been his biggest mistake. Maybe he should give up touring and go back to farming. Not goats, perhaps – they were too much trouble – but if he had a few cattle he would have to get up on his hind legs and go out and check on them at least once a day. There wasn't all that much money in farming, but he could do that as well as the fiddle-making. He looked down at the grass beneath his feet. His own winterage was useless, but this land up here was the finest winter grazing. It belonged to Mikey, and he let it out to Peter Hayes, but maybe they could come to some kind of arrangement. If JJ had cattle up here then he would have to walk up and see them every day, and at that moment he could think of no finer way to spend a couple of winter hours.

A vague feeling of guilt changed the direction of his thoughts. What was all that stuff about Mikey and the chopper? He tried to remember the conversation they'd had, but New Year's Eve was a long time ago. Surely he would never have promised to organize a helicopter? Mikey and Donal had clearly got the wrong end of the stick.

JJ stopped and his train of thought derailed. Ahead of him in the mist, just visible at the edge of his small circle of vision, a huge white goat was standing. Not *a* goat, but *that* goat. If, indeed, it was a goat. For a long moment JJ stood and stared at it. It stared back. JJ's mind returned to his visit to Tír na n'Óg twenty-five years ago, and the encounter he'd had there with a púca.

'Don't talk to any goats,' Aengus had warned him, so JJ hadn't talked to it, even when it changed its shape and towered over him, and asked him all kinds of questions. But that had been the wrong thing to do, he had discovered later, and Aengus had only been joking. It was dangerous, apparently, not to reply to a púca if you happened to have the misfortune of being addressed by one.

Was this the same goat he had met in Tír na n'Óg? It looked very similar. JJ cleared his throat but found it hard to speak. There was no one to see or hear him, but even so he felt self-conscious about talking to a goat. The whole thing was ridiculous. These hills were crawling with goats. Why should he suspect this one of being something different?

Because, he answered himself, he had seen it talking to Jenny yesterday. He cleared his throat again.

'Hello,' he said timidly.

The goat threw up its head and gave a sharp snort of alarm. For another moment it stared at JJ, then it turned and walked quickly away. Within seconds it was completely hidden by the mist.

JJ chuckled at his own absurd behaviour. He felt lighter, enormously relieved to discover that the goat was just a goat and nothing more. Until, that was, he heard the most extraordinary sound coming out of the mist from the direction that the goat had taken. It boomed all around him, bouncing back and forth inside the cloud like thunder. It might, just possibly, have been the bawling of a lonely goat, looking for its herd. But it sounded to JJ much more like a peal of sardonic laughter.

13

Between them Jenny and Donal found three shoes on their way home. None of them matched any other but two of them, Jenny was fairly sure, had partners in her room. The other one must have been out on the hillside for a very long time, because it was faded and bent and looked at least two sizes too small.

When they got in the first thing they saw was Hazel's enormous suitcase parked beside the front door. There were several plastic bags there as well, bulging with clothes and CDs and magazines. The sight of all that stuff made Jenny wonder if Hazel was leaving home for ever.

They went through into the kitchen, where Aisling was removing a tray of flapjacks from the oven and Aidan was screaming for a piece at the top of his lungs.

'No,' said Aisling. 'It's too hot.'

'Not too hot,' yelled Aidan. 'Give me one!'

Jenny handed him the twisted old shoe in an

attempt to divert his attention. He grabbed it and threw it very hard at Aisling. It hit her on the elbow. She gritted her teeth, picked up Aidan, all flailing fists and feet, and deposited him in the back yard. For a few minutes the rest of the family sat in a tense silence, weathering the storm of hammering and screaming on the other side of the locked door. Then Hazel said: 'Where's Dad?'

'He's coming home the long way,' said Donal.

'How long is the long way?' said Hazel, glancing at the clock. 'He was supposed to be driving me to the station.'

'Don't worry,' said Aisling. 'I can take you.'

'Typical, though, isn't it?' said Hazel. 'I'm going away for three months and he can't even be bothered to say goodbye.'

'He just forgot,' said Donal.

'That's even worse!' said Hazel.

'He might get here,' Aisling said in a calming voice. 'There's still half an hour or so.'

Aidan had stopped protesting and was now banging something metallic in the yard. Aisling looked out of the window to make sure it wasn't dangerous.

'We're going over to Mikey's,' Donal said.

'Both of you?' said Aisling. 'Jenny as well?' Donal nodded and she went on: 'That's nice. Mikey will love that.'

She was smiling, but Hazel's face had fallen. 'We'd better say goodbye, then,' she said. 'I'll be gone by the time you get back.'

She gave her brother a quick hug and a peck on the cheek, and then she turned to Jenny. 'Will you come up and visit me in Dublin?'

'No,' said Jenny, who couldn't stand the city.

To her surprise, Hazel's eyes filled with tears. 'This is goodbye, then,' she said, and flung her arms around Jenny, hugging her far more tightly than she ever had before. When she pulled back she looked Jenny in the eye and said: 'I'm sorry if I've been mean sometimes. You're the best sister in the world and I'm—' She was choked by a fresh wave of tears but she struggled on: 'I'm going to miss you so much!' She hugged the bewildered Jenny again, even longer and harder, sobbing all the while into her hairline.

Jenny knew she didn't understand this emotional stuff very well, but even so this seemed way over the top. She looked towards Aisling for some clue about how to behave, but to her astonishment Aisling's eyes were filled with tears as well, and she was wiping at them with the collar of her blouse. Jenny turned to Donal, but he was staring, with determined concentration, at the butter dish.

'Mummy!' called Aidan from outside, his voice filled with intense satisfaction. 'I broken it!'

Hazel at last let go of Jenny. Aisling laughed. 'It's only an old bucket,' she said, dabbing at what Jenny hoped were the last of her tears. 'Go on, you two. Get off down to Mikey's before it rains.'

They collected their instruments and walked down the driveway, across the New Line and through the fields beyond to Mikey's house. Neither of them said a word the whole way there. Jenny was trying to make sense of Hazel and, for a while, so was Donal. But he forgot about it sooner than she did and moved on to thinking about something else. Something he had seen, or thought he had seen, on the top of the beacon.

14

JJ was feeling a little less enthusiastic about his hill walk since the encounter with the goat. Although he was familiar with the broad table of the mountain top, everything looked different in the mist, and before another ten minutes had passed he realized that he had lost his bearings. He had passed by the crossed walls, which had been built for sheltering cattle some time in the previous century and were, he knew, the most recent stone structure up there. That meant that the two small cairns ought to have come into view shortly afterwards, but they hadn't. They might be just out of sight, shrouded in the mist, but they might not be. Perhaps he had not come far enough yet?

He walked on for another couple of hundred metres until he came to a hollow in the ground, bordered on two sides by little escarpments of limestone, like natural walls. Inside it was a jumble of loose stones that might once have been some kind of human shelter. The grass in the bottom of the basin was greener than the other hilltop grasses, and JJ could see that the soil, where it had been exposed by grubbing badgers, was rich and dark. It was quite a distinctive feature of the landscape and that fact made JJ uneasy, because he didn't remember ever having seen it before.

There was something very attractive about the formation and its promise of shelter from the gales that lashed across these hills and caused the few stunted blackthorns that survived them to grow almost parallel to the ground, with all their sparse branches pointing east. JJ was practically certain that the place must have been a little settlement at some time. He could almost sense the presence of those small, hardy people in the air around him, like ghosts in the mist.

He sat on the damp rock at the lip of the hollow and thought about Jenny. Why had he been so hard on her? He knew that púcas existed: he had met one twenty-five years ago and he may have just met one again. Fairies existed as well, and one of them was his grandfather. So why not ghosts as well? He ought to have listened to Jenny instead of taking that juvenile, sneering tone. And he should have asked her straight out, in a perfectly natural way, whether or not the white goat was a púca. That was what a good parent would have done.

JJ feared that he was not a very good parent. He was afraid that Aisling was right when she charged him with being absent-minded and feckless. Sometimes, with a secret pride, he blamed it on his fairy blood, but he knew that was no excuse. His mother had twice as much fairy blood as he had and she was the most hard-working and well-organized person he knew. Perhaps it had been the visit to Tír na n'Óg that had caused it. Perhaps he had caught fecklessness from the fairies, like a disease.

He looked around him, wishing that the cloud would hurry up and find its way back into the sky. He would, he decided, give Coleman's church a miss. Its ruined walls were tucked away in the fringes of the hazel woods that ran along the base of Eagle's Rock, and it was in exactly that place, on the other side of the time skin in Tír na n'Óg, that he had first met the púca. Instead he would skirt the woods and cut straight across to the Carron road and walk home from there.

But when he stood up he realized that he had absolutely no idea how to get there. He couldn't even remember which direction he had come from. If he went the wrong way he could be wandering around for hours before he met a road. On the other hand, if he sat and waited for the cloud to lift he might be here for days.

It was then that he remembered, with a shock, that he had promised to drive Hazel to the station. He cursed the mist, himself, and his fairy grandfather, took a wild guess and began walking rapidly across the rough ground. He passed a couple of stone piles, but nothing he recognized until, after about twenty minutes, he made out the squat, conical form of the beacon over to his left. What was more, the children were still there.

Or at least, he could have sworn he saw one of them standing on the top. But when he got there, the beacon was deserted and utterly, anciently silent.

Hazel was just dragging her case across the yard to the car when she spotted her father careering down the hillside above the house. She laughed and pointed him out to Aidan.

'Goat,' said Aidan.

'It's not a goat,' said Hazel. 'It's Daddy.'

'Goat,' said Aidan. 'There!'

And sure enough he was right. Higher on the slope, just below the level of the cloud which was obscuring the top of the mountain, a big white goat was standing with its front feet on a boulder. It was a long distance away, but Hazel had the distinct impression that it was watching every step of her father's precipitous descent.

15

Nancy McGrath got shopping for Mikey whenever he needed it, and her car was just pulling away as Donal and Jenny arrived.

'Whatever happened to your shoes, girleen?' said Mikey.

'I left them at home,' said Jenny.

'She never wears them,' said Donal, not sure whether this sounded like a defence of Jenny or a condemnation, and not sure, either, which it was meant to be.

Mikey was leaning against the dresser, waiting for the kettle to boil. 'Well, you should wear them,' he said. 'You're lucky to have them.'

Jenny traced a pattern on the oilskin tablecloth with the mouthpiece of her whistle.

'My feet can't see where they're going when they have shoes on them,' she said.

'Is that right?' said Mikey. 'All the same, you should

wear them. I was never without shoes and nor was my father, but there were people in this parish in his day that couldn't afford to have shoes. I thought you were a little ghost from them days when you came in the door.'

Donal seized the unexpected opportunity. 'Do you believe in ghosts, Mikey?

'I do, begod,' said Mikey, without hesitation. 'I usedn't to, but these days I do.'

'Have you ever seen one?'

The kettle had boiled but Mikey ignored it. 'Well,' he said, 'that depends on what you mean by "seen". You can't see a ghost the way you can see you or me. You can't look straight at them, like. You just—' He stopped, aware of the wide-eyed, earnest gazes of the two children. 'Sure, what am I on about?' he went on. 'Pay no attention to me, now, you hear? I'm getting soft in the head in my old age.'

He turned and poured water into the teapot to warm it.

'You can only see them out of the corner of your eye, can't you?' said Donal seriously.

Mikey put the teapot down and turned to face him. He reached for a chair-back to support himself; missed it the first time, caught it the second.

'Come here to me,' he said, in the sternest voice

Donal had ever heard him use. 'Did your father ever say anything more about that helicopter?'

Donal coloured, embarrassed by JJ. 'I think he forgot,' he said.

'And did you remind him?'

Donal nodded. He wanted to tell Mikey what JJ had told him; that he was only messing and had never really meant it, but he couldn't find the courage.

'Good man!' said Mikey, his spirits visibly rising.

'But you should talk to him about it yourself,' said Donal hurriedly. 'Why don't you phone him?'

'I will,' said Mikey, turning back to the teapot. 'Now. What about a tune?'

When Donal and Jenny got back home a couple of hours later, they found JJ frantically trying to organize musicians for the céilí that night. Since most of his big tours happened during the summer, the house dances ran from September to May and then stopped for three months. The last one of the season was happening that evening, and JJ had forgotten about it until now. He and Hazel normally played fiddle, with Aisling backing them on the electric keyboard, and, more often than not, his mother Helen would come down from Dublin and join them on the concertina.

'Why didn't she come down and then take Hazel back with her tomorrow?' he asked Aisling.

'Why didn't you ask her to?' she answered.

She took Aidan with her and went off to organize the food and drink, and JJ got on the phone to Flo Fahy, who was delighted to come along and join him with her concertina. And so it was that the céilí, like every céilí that had ever been held at the Liddy house, turned out to be a resounding success.

16

Jenny didn't think the archaeologists would work on a Sunday, but she went up to the beacon anyway, just in case. She waited for a couple of hours, even though it was pouring with rain, and when she was certain that they weren't going to come she joined the púca at the edge of the mountain and together they descended into the woods.

It was the púca who had told Jenny that she was wasting her time at school. The sum of human knowledge, he told her, was getting smaller and smaller, and school was one of the main reasons for this. The human habit of imprisoning their children in learning factories led to them being overloaded with information and deprived of experience. The study of nature had been reduced to an occasional discretionary ramble and, cut off from its source, human life was fast becoming safe, sterile and completely meaningless. Jenny only understood about half of what the púca said, but that half was enough. What he taught her made far more sense than what they tried to teach her at school.

Like the ghost. It was the púca who had told her about him and how she would be able to see him if she sat still for long enough and waited. It was the púca who had taught her how to be comfortable in the cold and wet, and that human intolerance for wild weather was a mental, not a physical problem. And it was the púca, that May Sunday, who taught her how to see the wind.

Goats, he explained, could see the weather on the wind. That was why they were always in the right place at the right time, always sheltered when they needed to be. People, if they were taught properly, could see it, too. But that wasn't all that could be done. An assiduous reader of the wind could tell a great deal about the world, and many other things besides.

He would begin by teaching her to see the coarse winds; those which moved in simple time across the surface of things and pushed the weather fronts from place to place. They were relatively easy to see, and before too long Jenny should be able to forecast not only the upcoming weather but more long-term things, such as the optimal growing and harvesting times and the probable movement of fish and bird nations in their migrations around the globe.

Then, if and when she was proficient at that, the púca would teach her to see the winds of change, which also moved on the surface of things, and in simple time. They could show her the trends that were affecting not only humankind but all life on the planet, whether animal or vegetable. They were blowing sour these days, he said, and they had been for some considerable time, but he hoped they would sweeten again before much longer.

After that, if Jenny passed muster with those ones, he would try and show her the winds that travelled across complex time. These were the stellar winds, which blew from one side of the universe to the other and took all the short cuts through space and time, and the subtle winds which crossed between worlds, as well as within and without, behind and betwixt, above and below and beyond.

It was somewhere around there that Jenny lost the plot and the púca decided it was time to move from the theoretical to the practical. He gave her a first short lesson and sent her home.

'Bad storm tomorrow,' she told Donal when she got home.

'That's not what the weather forecast says,' said Donal.

17

The day wasn't stormy. It wasn't even raining.

'Bit more practice,' said Jenny to the púca as they climbed up the hillside at first light, and the púca agreed. He left her at the top of the series of steep escarpments that JJ called the stony steps, and she went on alone to the beacon.

The ghost was where he always was, standing on a tiny level spot about a metre from the summit stone. As Jenny approached she remembered that the reason the púca had told her how to see him was so that she could rescue him; set him free from the vow that bound him to the hill of stones. She hadn't the faintest idea how she would do it. The last time she had asked the púca about it he had told her to just keep talking to him. 'Be his friend,' he had said. 'That's the first thing.' So that was what she had done, and it hadn't occurred to her before now to ask what the second thing might be.

Not for the first time she found herself trying to imagine the vast expanses of time that the ghost had passed in that same spot. If no one rescued him, would he really stay there for ever? She wondered where the other people went, all the millions of ghosts who hadn't made a vow that they would stay. There was a lot of talk in school about heaven and hell, but JJ and Aisling weren't religious and they encouraged all the children to ignore that stuff. But the ghost was proof that something continued after death, and if the others didn't go to heaven or to hell, then where did they go?

She sat down on a stone. The ghost was very quiet today, and she thought of telling him about seeing the wind, but she changed her mind. He might ask her where she had learned to do it, and the púca was insistent that Jenny didn't tell the ghost about her friendship with him. He said the ghost might ask to see him, but he said he remembered the time when the boy was alive, and he couldn't bear to see him now, in the sad state he was in.

'Are you that old?' Jenny had asked the púca.

'I'm that old,' the púca had said, 'and a lot more as well.'

So Jenny said nothing, but sat beside the ghost and practised watching the wind, and waited for the archaeologists.

* * *

114

'I could go up and get her,' said JJ to Aisling. 'She'll be a bit late but I'd say I could have her in school by eleven.'

Aisling sighed. 'Oh, what difference does it make, JJ? What's the point in sending her to school anyway? She won't need it where she's going.'

'Where is she going?' asked Donal, coming into the kitchen with his school bag.

'Um—' said JJ.

'Um—' said Aisling. 'Well, all I meant is that she'll learn a lot more from watching the archaeologists than she would in school.'

'For a day,' added JJ.

'Great,' said Donal, lobbing his school bag into the corner. 'Then so will I. I'm going up there, too.'

Aisling and JJ exchanged glances, but they knew they had walked themselves into it.

'OK,' said JJ. 'Let's have breakfast and then I'll go up there with you.'

'Nope,' said Aisling decisively. 'You can stay here for a change and mind Mister Tantrum. It's my turn for a jaunt.'

Donal reached for the cereals. He was pleased enough with the result of that little exchange, but he wasn't fooled by the answer he'd got. All those tears yesterday and now this.

Something was up.

18

Alice Kelly was astonished to discover that the little girl was there again, sitting on the top of the barrow. There were no two ways about it – she was going to have to leave. Apart from anything else, the barrow would become unstable when they began moving stones. It was not a safe place for anybody, and she was not about to take any chances with a schoolchild.

Alice unlocked the flimsy little padlocks at the bottom of the tent zippers and inspected the interiors. Nothing had been touched. At least the girl wasn't a thief. While she waited for the others to arrive she put on a kettle for some coffee and made the first official entry in the excavation log. It was only a date and a time, but it marked the beginning and Alice was filled with delicious anticipation.

By nine thirty she had finished her coffee and washed her mug, using the bare minimum of water. David Connelly and the students still hadn't arrived, despite the joint decision that they should all be present and ready to begin work at nine o'clock sharp. Their funding was only good for fourteen weeks, and every single moment was precious. Becoming more irritated by the second, Alice zipped up the tent and surveyed the mountain top. The white goat was there again, in the distance, but the only person in sight was that wretched little girl. Allowing her irritation to get the better of her, Alice strode to the foot of the barrow.

'Why aren't you in school?' she demanded.

Jenny remembered what the púca had said about factories and information and experience. She decided, on reflection, that the issue was too technical for an easy answer.

'Lost your tongue?' snapped Alice Kelly.

'No,' said Jenny. 'And I haven't lost my temper, either.'

'What is that supposed to mean?' said the archae-ologist, though in fact she knew perfectly well what it meant and was quite taken aback. When Jenny made no reply she went on, a little less aggressively: 'Well, anyway, you can't stay there. We're going to start moving the stones soon, and then it won't be safe up there.'

To her astonishment the child grinned broadly. 'That's OK,' she said. 'When you start moving the stones I'll come down.'

Alice turned away, infuriated by the girl's wilfulness. She was further infuriated by the sight of the rest of her party, arriving at last but strolling quite casually across the mountain top as though they had all the time in the world. She set out to meet them and hustle them along.

Jenny watched, sensing the ghost at her side watching too. He had told her before that although he could see quite clearly he couldn't see very far – a couple of hundred metres at the very most. He had told her that it was a disappointment to him that he couldn't see as far as the ocean, or the mountains to either side of that one, or to the sister beacon on the next hill along the coast. That one did hold a burial chamber, he said, unlike this one. He wished the archaeologists would go there instead.

He had also told her that, in all the time he had stood guard over the beacon, it had only been threatened once. A group of men had come and tried to move the stones. He had prevented them from doing so and they had gone away again. That had been his only entertainment in three thousand years. And now he was about to get a bit more.

Alice Kelly returned with her team. One of the students complained that he was gasping for a cup of coffee, but all he got was a reprimand. After a brief discussion about where the stones were to be piled, the team put on their work gloves and moved in.

'Come on, now,' said Alice to Jenny. 'Down you get.'

'You haven't moved any stones yet,' said Jenny.

'No, but we're going to.'

'I don't think so.'

'Look,' said Alice crossly. 'I'm very tired of your little games. This is an archaeological site and not a play-ground. It isn't a safe place for children. Please come down, this instant.'

'I will,' said Jenny. 'As soon as you've moved the first stone.'

'Right!' snapped Alice. Bristling with fury, she bent to lift a small rock near the base of the barrow. But something very peculiar happened. As she put her hand on the stone she seemed to lose her balance. She staggered, tried to straighten up, then sat down heavily on the ground.

'Are you all right?' said David Connelly.

'I think so,' said Alice. 'I just got a sudden dizzy spell.' She stood up, apparently quite steady again, but when she bent towards the barrow, reaching for a different stone this time, the very same thing happened again.

Alice Kelly was confident about the state of her health. She was well into her sixties but she was a robust hill-walker and prided herself on her ability to work long hours on digs in all kinds of weather conditions without any ill effects.

'I'm probably overstressed,' she said, a little shame-facedly. 'You carry on while I take a breather.'

David Connelly and two of the students stepped forward to take her place, and Jenny looked on as the scene moved from mild comedy to high farce. The archaeologists swayed and lurched and stumbled and tumbled. Time and again they stepped back to clear their spinning heads. Time and again they came back for another try, and always with the same result. Beside her, Jenny was aware of the ghost's fierce concentration, but also of his enjoyment. She didn't know how he was doing it but it was, she thought, a great trick.

It wasn't long before the archaeologists tired and retreated, realizing it was useless. But Alice Kelly wasn't defeated yet. While the others stood and shook their heads in bewilderment, she strode back to the foot of the beacon.

'It's you, isn't it?' she shouted.

'Are you talking to me?' said Jenny innocently.

'Who else would I be talking to?' Alice was shaking with anger and practically screaming now. 'You're doing this, aren't you?'

'I'm not,' said Jenny, finally becoming intimidated by the force of Alice Kelly's fury. She wasn't prone to feelings of guilt but she did have a sense of self-preservation. 'I told you before. It's the ghost.'

'What nonsense! Now will you please come down from there and let us get on with our work.'

'But I'm not stopping you,' said Jenny.

Alice's voice reached its highest pitch yet. 'Will you please just do as you are told!'

'Is there a problem here?'

Jenny looked round. Aisling and Donal had arrived, approaching the barrow from the blind side, away from all the activity.

'Hi, Mum,' said Jenny brightly. 'What are you doing here?'

'We came up to have a look at the dig,' said Aisling.

'There isn't one,' said Jenny.

'Is this your daughter?' said Alice Kelly, making a visible attempt to get her temper under control. 'Could you please get her to come down from there? She's obstructing us in our work.'

'Oh, Jenny,' said Aisling. 'Why are you doing that?'

'I'm not,' said Jenny, but she came down anyway, more to prove her point than anything else.

'What was she doing, exactly?' Aisling asked.

'She was . . . well . . . she was . . .'

David Connelly came to her rescue.

'Would you excuse us, please?' he said to Aisling. 'We're just about to take a coffee break.'

19

JJ parked Aidan in front of the television, even though he had often criticized Aisling for doing the same thing. Somehow he still hadn't got round to finishing off Sean Pearce's fiddle and there was plenty more to be done once that was off the bench. He rummaged around in his box of bits until he found the right tail-piece, then opened a new packet of strings and began fitting them. That was as far as he got before Aidan became bored with the television and came, full tilt, to find him.

'No, Aidan,' said JJ sternly. 'Not in here.'

'Why?' said Aidan.

'Why' was because the workshop was filled to the rafters with delicate musical instruments, fragile bows and tools that were not only expensive and precious but also lethally sharp. None of the children were allowed in there.

'Out of bounds,' said JJ.

'Not out of brown,' said Aidan. 'Can I do it?'

He lunged at the fiddle in JJ's hands and almost knocked him off his stool.

'No, Aidan!' JJ held the fiddle at arm's length. 'Daddy's working. Go and watch the TV.'

'I want to work,' said Aidan. 'Let me do it!'

Aidan grabbed the soundpost setter from the tool rack and began stabbing Sean Pearce's brand-new violin case with it. JJ took it off him. Aidan kicked the violin case and was just about to jump on it when JJ whisked him up off the floor, carried him out into the kitchen and locked the workshop door behind them.

'Come on,' he said. 'We'll do something else instead.'

'What?' said Aidan suspiciously.

JJ looked around at the cluttered kitchen. A thorough clear-up was badly needed.

'I don't know,' he said. 'What do you want to do?'

20

When the archaeologists finished their coffee break they were irritated to discover that the woman and her two children were still there.

'This isn't a public exhibition,' Alice Kelly said to Aisling. 'There's nothing here for you to see.'

'We're not doing any harm,' said Aisling.

'We're going to be moving some big stones,' said Alice. 'It could be dangerous.'

'Be careful, then,' said Aisling. She took her mobile out of her pocket and showed it to her. 'I'll phone for a helicopter if one of them falls on you.'

Alice glared at her. 'Shouldn't those children be in school?'

'Yes,' said Aisling. 'But I thought it would be educational for them to see a professional dig. One of them might like to become an archaeologist one day.'

Maureen, the girl who had brought Jenny a cup of coffee, gave all three of them a sympathetic smile.

Then she joined her team leaders at the base of the barrow to make a fresh attempt on the stones.

Donal was looking at Aisling's mobile. 'Can you really do that?' he said. 'Phone for a chopper?'

'Well, if someone was injured I could dial nine-nine-nine and the emergency services would probably send one,' she said. 'How else would they get someone down from up here?'

Donal nodded. 'But you can't just phone for one like you'd phone for a taxi?'

Aisling laughed. 'Actually, some people do. Very rich people. Remember the one we saw at the Weir in Kilcolgan last year? Someone hired that one to bring them out from Galway to the restaurant there.'

Donal nodded thoughtfully. 'How much would it cost, do you think?'

Aisling puffed out her cheeks and blew air. 'I don't know. Hundreds, I imagine. Silly money.'

Donal looked over at the archaeologists, who had begun to behave very strangely. The older woman was sitting on the ground with her head between her knees. The man with the binoculars had rolled a big chunk of rock a few centimetres down the side of the beacon, then collapsed in a heap on top of it. The girl who had smiled at them reached for a smaller stone, then sank to her knees and keeled over sideways.

Donal looked at his mother, who was snorting with

restrained laughter. Jenny was giving a thumbs-up sign to the thin air at the top of the mound – to the ghost, he assumed. Behind her he could see his father, with Aidan perched on his shoulders, striding over the hillside on his way to join them.

The archaeologists gathered their wits and retreated again. They stood, looking dazed, a few metres away. Alice Kelly turned to Aisling, her face flushed with anger and humiliation.

'Look, I'm sorry,' she said, 'but I really do have to ask you to leave.'

'Is there a problem here?' said JJ, appearing at Aisling's side.

All five of the archaeologists stared at him as if he had two heads. Actually, he had, but he detached one of them and put it, along with the rest of Aidan, on the ground.

Alice Kelly couldn't believe her eyes. This dig was about as far off the beaten track as it was possible to get in a place as small as Ireland. It was supposed to have been a pleasure; a few months of healthy labour out in the open air, with the added possibility of an exciting discovery at the end of it. Instead it was turning into a disaster. Not only was some weird phenomenon holding up the work, but the place was as busy as a railway station.

'Yes,' she said to JJ, with icy calm. 'There is indeed

a problem.' She pointed at Jenny. 'This child here is doing something to me and my crew and it's stopping us from doing our work.'

'What is she doing to you?' said JJ.

'She's . . . She's making us dizzy.'

'Dizzy?' said JJ. 'You don't have that kind of power, do you, Jenny?'

'No,' said Jenny. 'But the ghost does.'

'That sounds more likely,' said JJ. He turned back to Alice Kelly and said, in a stage-Irish accent, 'I'd say it's the ghost, Mrs.'

Aisling couldn't contain her laughter any longer. It exploded out of her and she turned away and hid her face in her hands.

'Mum!' said Donal sharply. 'Shh!'

But it was too late. Aisling's laughter tipped Alice Kelly over the edge, and she lost it.

'Get out of here!' she shrieked, her voice blistering her larynx. 'Just leave us alone!'

She turned on her heel and stormed away towards the tents. Aidan, who was clambering around on the lower skirts of the beacon, picked up a fist-sized stone and tossed it after her. He fell down immediately afterwards, but this was because he was two and a half and wearing large wellingtons, and not because he was dizzy. It sent Aisling into renewed gales of laughter.

David Connelly drew in a deep breath and came

over to where the rest of the family were standing.

'I'm sorry about this,' he said, as good-naturedly as he could, 'but it's not a good time for you to be visiting the dig. Perhaps if you came back in a few days' time . . . ?'

'Good enough,' said JJ. 'We're just down at the bottom of the hill if you need anything. Cup of tea. Aspirin. Psychiatrist.'

He picked up Aidan, who went into automatic rage mode, and the others followed them, slightly reluctantly, towards the stony steps and home.

JJ walked beside Jenny. 'Well?' he said. 'Was it you that was making them dizzy?'

'No,' said Jenny. 'How would I be able to make them dizzy?'

JJ shrugged. 'You never know with you, Jenny. I've no idea what you might be able to do.'

Jenny was bewildered. 'Could you make someone dizzy, then?'

'Me?' said JJ. 'Apart from the adoring fans who flock to my concerts?' He shook his head. 'No, I couldn't. But I'm not like you.'

He scrubbed the top of her head with a big, rough hand and pulled her close for a side-by-side hug. Aidan seized his chance and took a swing at her head with the blue wellington he had taken off in the hope of just such an opportunity. It hit her, but not very hard. JJ took it off him. In a fit of pique, Aidan pulled off the other one and hurled it down the first of the stony steps just ahead of them. It landed in front of Donal, who was climbing down. He picked it up and turned to his mother, who was just behind him.

'How much money do I have in the Credit Union?' he asked her.

'I'm not sure without checking your savings book,' she said. 'Somewhere around three hundred euros, I'd say. Why?'

Donal shrugged. 'Just wondering,' he said.

21

When they'd had lunch Jenny went out again, after promising not to go anywhere near the archaeologists. Aisling and Aidan went off in the car to do the weekly supermarket shop, and JJ went back to work on the fiddles. As soon as he was sure that the coast was clear, Donal got out the Golden Pages and began hunting. There was no listing under 'Helicopters', but when he looked it up in the index at the back it was there.

Helicopters – See Aircraft Charter & Hire.

He turned to the page and found no fewer than four listings for helicopters, all of them offering 'chartered customer services' and, for some reason, 'golf trips'. Donal put his finger on the first number and looked at the phone. He took several deep breaths before he lifted the receiver and several more before he dialled.

'Hello?' said a woman's voice at the other end of the line.

'Hello,' said Donal, trying to make his voice sound deep and adult. 'I want to hire a helicopter.'

There was a little silence and Donal realized the voice thing wasn't working. Then the woman said, 'Who is this speaking, please?'

'Donal Liddy. It's about a present. For . . . for my grandfather.'

'I see,' said the woman. 'And where does your grandfather want to go?'

'To the top of Sliabh Carron,' said Donal.

'The top of where?'

'Sliabh Carron. It's a mountain. In The Burren.'

'I'm sorry, Mr Liddy,' said the woman. 'We're not licensed to land on the top of mountains.'

'It's very flat up there,' said Donal anxiously. 'It would be dead easy to land.'

'We can only use helipads or approved and inspected sites,' said the woman. 'Perhaps there's somewhere else your grandfather would like to go? We specialize in golf trips. I'm sure he'd enjoy one of those.'

Donal tried to imagine Mikey on a golf course, with little success. 'How much would a golf trip cost?' he asked.

'Well, we have packages beginning at four and a half

thousand, including five-star hotel accommodation and course fees.'

'I'll have a think about it,' said Donal.

When he put down the receiver his hand was shaking. He waited until it had stopped, then rang the other companies. One woman insisted on talking to his parents, and when Donal said they weren't there she hung up on him. The other two people, both men, had similar stories to the first one. They didn't land on mountains. They offered golf trips.

In desperation, Donal phoned the air-sea rescue number, but all he got for that was a flea in his ear for wasting emergency services' time. He wandered into the kitchen and hunted for biscuits. He was bitterly disappointed by the results of his efforts, but at least this put an end to the matter. He would tell Mikey that JJ had tried his hardest to get him a chopper but there was no way it could be done. He dreaded seeing the old man's face when he gave him that news. He wished he could be like his dad, and just not worry about these things.

It was true that JJ wasn't worrying about Mikey and the chopper, but he was quite worried about the ghost. On the way down the hillside he had asked Jenny about it and she had told him all she could. What bothered JJ the most was the bit about the monsters.

Jenny had hunched her shoulders and made grizzly bear arms and a gruesome, snarling face. They were very big, she had told him, and they wanted the chopper, but she couldn't be more specific than that.

'And do you think the ghost can keep out the archaeologists?' he had asked.

'Definitely,' said Jenny. 'No bother to him. He could do a lot worse to them if he wanted to, but he likes them. He likes everybody.'

But now JJ was worried. How determined would they be, he wondered, to get to the bottom of it? He doubted they would go to the lengths of dynamiting the thing, but what if they airlifted in one of those small mechanical diggers? Would the ghost be able to stop a machine?

He finished stringing up Sean Pearce's fiddle and played a couple of tunes on it. It was OK, but he'd like a bit more power in the higher ranges. He loosened the strings and reached for the soundpost setter. It wasn't in the rack. He remembered taking it away from Aidan, but not where he had put it. He was in the kitchen hunting for it when Donal came in.

'Dad?' he said, and did his trick of waiting until he had JJ's full attention. 'Do you think someone could make it up to the beacon on a donkey?'

'You possibly could,' said JJ. 'But when was the last time you saw a donkey around here?'

Donal thought about it. The answer was that he had never seen one around there. Nor had he ever seen anyone riding one anywhere in Ireland.

'Why?' JJ asked.

Donal sighed. 'Just wondering,' he said.

22

Jenny was determined to pay another visit to the dig on Tuesday, but she was collared by JJ at five thirty in the morning and kept under close observation until it was time to go to school. She tried two appeals, one on the grounds of a sudden desire to become an archaeologist and the other on the grounds of an equally sudden attack of belly-ache, but no one was buying either excuse.

So she spent the day in school, trying with all her might to make the teacher feel dizzy. The only results were two reprimands for staring, the first one quite mild and the second one extremely savage.

The minute she got home she kicked off her shoes and raced away across the pastureland and up the mountainside. When she got to the beacon the scene was deserted, but she noticed that the marker strings had all been moved around to the other side, as though the archaeologists had decided to try a different approach.

After school on the following day she was just about to head up the mountain again when there was a knock at the front door. Aisling opened it and found Alice Kelly and David Connelly standing there in the rain. She invited them in. They declined the offer of tea and waited, somewhat anxiously, in the sitting room while Donal winkled JJ out of the workshop.

When everyone had gathered, Alice Kelly began. 'I wanted to apologize. I behaved, very badly when you came up to visit the dig and I hope you'll forgive me.'

'You're grand,' said JJ. 'We understand.'

'Absolutely,' said Aisling, fighting off a renewed desire to laugh.

Alice turned to Jenny, but Jenny hadn't actually heard anything she had said because she was too busy trying to make her get dizzy and fall over again.

'The thing is,' she went on, 'that none of us had ever encountered anything like what happened to us up there. It was quite frightening and disorientating. I overreacted and blamed your daughter, which was clearly ridiculous.'

'Clearly,' JJ agreed.

David Connelly took over and explained what had happened to them all when they tried to move the stones. They had made several more attempts on that day, and more again on Tuesday, at different points around the base of the barrow. The same thing had happened to them every time. Eventually, on Wednesday, one of the students had hit upon the idea of seeing what would happen if, instead of trying to take stones away from the pile, they tried to add some. The results had been quite remarkable. They had been able to move around freely on the slopes carrying the imported stones, but once they had put them down among the others they were entirely unable to remove them again.

'So that was when we decided to call it a day,' David finished up.

'But we wondered if your daughter—' Alice Kelly began.

'Jenny,' said Aisling.

'Jenny,' said Alice. 'We wondered if Jenny would mind telling us a little bit more about the . . . er . . .'

'The ghost?' said JJ.

So Jenny told them, cautiously, a few things. She told them how to see the ghost and how he had met his death, and that he was guarding the beacon against intruders. She told them how much he loved the human race, and how pleased he was to see people up there on the mountain. But she didn't tell them about the chopper in case it made them want to dig it up, and she didn't make the monster shape and do the gruesome face, either. The archaeologists listened politely, and seemed contented enough with what she told them.

'So what will you do now?' JJ asked.

'We were wondering,' said David, 'whether Jenny happens to know anything about the other barrow. The one on the next hill.'

Jenny nodded enthusiastically. 'There's no ghost on that one,' she said.

'Are you sure?' said Alice Kelly.

'Positive,' said Jenny. 'And there is someone buried under it. It's a much better place for digging.'

Alice looked pleased. 'We'll move our operations over there, then.'

'And will you publish what you've discovered?' said JJ.

'No,' said Alice. 'The entire team has been sworn to secrecy. If word of this got out we would have half the country marching around up there, trying to get a look at the ghost, and ruining the barrow. That would be in nobody's interests.'

'But you'll come back to it at some stage?' said JJ.

'Perhaps,' said Alice. 'But I very much doubt it.'

Jenny raced up to the beacon. When she got there she found that the markers were gone, and so were the tents. The only things left were the twelve white plastic containers, their contents now of absolutely no use to anyone. Jenny was sorry to have missed the fun but she was pleased that the ghost had kept the beacon safe. She went up and sat with him, and complimented him on his achievement, and told him what the archaeologists had said to her. But instead of being proud or satisfied he seemed gloomier than ever. The archaeologists had been nice. He liked having people around, and he missed them. He had to stop them, it was true, but the beasts were the real problem. He showed them to Jenny again, and she shuddered at the terrifying images that invaded her mind. They were taller than the beacon. They had massive thighs and long, scaly snouts, and enormous, twisted horns.

'Stop it,' she said to the ghost, and he did. The visions faded from Jenny's mind and the fear passed, but she was unsettled and she didn't want to stay there any longer. She stood up unsteadily, picked her way down the hill of jumbled stones and set out for home.

On the way she met the púca, and they dropped into the woods, where they could talk without being seen, and where the púca could adopt his long, almost human form. He spoke more clearly that way, because his face was flatter and his tongue was rounder. But he had no lessons for her that day. He wanted to know what was happening up on top.

Jenny told him about the departure of the archaeologists and he seemed pleased.

'Perhaps we've seen the last of them,' he said. 'Perhaps that poor ghost could be persuaded to give up his foolishness now and move on.'

'The archaeologists said they might come back,' said Jenny. 'And anyway, it isn't them he's worried about. Not really. It's the monsters.'

The púca shook his wise old head, slowly. 'What monsters?' he said.

Jenny gave the best description she could of the beasts the ghost had shown her. 'And have you seen them?' said the púca.

'Only in my mind,' said Jenny. 'The way he showed them to me.'

'And where does he say they live, these monsters?' said the púca.

Jenny shrugged. 'He doesn't say.'

'Doesn't he?' said the púca. 'But they must be somewhere. You have walked all over these hills. You've been into the woods and the hollows and the valleys. Have you ever seen a monster like that?'

'No,' said Jenny.

'No,' said the púca. 'And that poor boy needs to be persuaded that there's no need for him to spend eternity standing on that hill. Because he's badly deluded, Jenny. It's all in his head.'

'You mean he's making it all up?'

The púca nodded. 'Not on purpose, of course. But it isn't so unusual, you know, for someone to believe in something that isn't true.'

Jenny shook her head in bewilderment. 'You mean he's been standing up there for thousands of years, guarding the beacon against . . . against nothing?'

'Well,' said the púca, 'what do you think?'

Jenny looked around at the hills and across the plain to the ocean. 'I think you're right,' she said. 'I think there are no monsters.'

JUNE

1

'Do you ever feel that you don't fit in?' the púca said to Jenny one day.

'I feel that all the time,' said Jenny.

'Maybe it's because it's true,' he said. 'Not everyone who lives in this world belongs to it, you know. There are many other worlds, and sometimes mistakes happen. People slip through.'

He told her about the Cat-heads and the Dog-heads who had both, on separate occasions, broken through into this world and tried to devour it, because the places they inhabited were so mean and hungry. He told her about dark worlds where light never shone and about the creatures which lived there, and about the senses they used to track each other down so that they could eat each other. He told her about a world whose inhabitants didn't eat each other at all, but ate pure light and shone like glow-worms.

Jenny listened, but she didn't feel she belonged to any of those worlds.

There were huge worlds, tiny worlds, worlds within worlds. The púca told her about many of them, and he told her, finally, about the nearest one to this one; the kingdom of the fairy folk, which is called Tír na n'Óg, or the land of eternal youth. He told her how the sun never stopped shining in that world, because there was no time there to persuade it to move on. He told her about the unworried, unhurried people who lived there, and about their music and their dancing, and about the Dagda, their king, who had control over the fluid wall that protected his people from time. But he didn't tell her, for reasons of his own, about how this strange world and its inhabitants were intimately connected with her.

2

JJ left on the seventh of June for a six-week tour of Japan and the USA. Before he left he took over the running of the house while Aisling went up to Dublin and spent a week with her in-laws and Hazel.

She had badly needed that break, and although she had only been back for a few days she felt as though she already needed another one. Aidan was still making the most of the 'terrible twos' and Jenny was as dreamy and unreliable as ever. But that was not why Aisling called the police. Calling the police was another part of JJ's master plan.

It was about nine thirty on a damp evening. Although it wasn't really getting dark yet, low, heavy clouds made it seem as though it was.

'My daughter's missing,' she told the duty officer who answered the phone. 'She went out walking this afternoon and she didn't come home for her dinner.'

The guard took all the details. He asked how old

Jenny was and whether she had ever gone wandering off before. Aisling told him that she was eleven, and that she often went walking around and about but that she was afraid something must have happened to her this time, because she was out so late.

The duty officer said he would send someone round to the house, but by the time the Garda car arrived, Jenny had come home.

Aisling apologized profusely. The guards were sympathetic and told the bewildered Jenny not to be frightening her mother like that. Aisling saw them out, then stood leaning against the front door, shaking with guilt and anxiety. She couldn't believe it was ever going to work. The whole plan was insane.

3

'Did you ever wonder,' said the púca, 'how it is that human beings have become so plentiful? In almost every other one of the myriad worlds there is harmony and balance between the plants and the creatures that inhabit them. They eat each other, of course, but that is natural. And it is also natural that if any one species looks like becoming too successful and dominant then we step in to correct the balance.'

'We?' said Jenny.

'We have been called many things, but you don't want a list of names, do you? Nature-gods is possibly the most accurate description of us. Would you be happy with that?'

'I suppose so,' said Jenny.

'It was several thousand years ago that things began to go wrong in this world,' said the púca. 'From the beginnings of time, we were the only gods human beings had ever known, and they respected us and obeyed our laws, and cared for every living thing that grew on the planet. They ate other creatures of course, but that is only natural, and part of the scheme of things that we had devised.' He shook his head ruefully. 'A lovely place it was. One of the loveliest. Until the fairies came along.'

'The fairies?' said Jenny. 'From Tír na n'Óg?'

The púca shuddered. 'The same,' he said. 'They came across into this world with their magic and their music, and the human race fell under their spell. They abandoned us, and adopted the fairies as their gods.'

He paused to pluck a wild strawberry leaf and for a while he chewed on it thoughtfully.

'They lost respect for us and began to flout our laws. They started to cut down forests for their cooking fires and their huts and to clear space for grazing their herds. They began to spread out and multiply at an alarming rate. Taking over the place, essentially. We used all our power to get the human race back under control, but the fairy folk liked being worshipped, and they protected the human race with their magic. Eventually the state of the world got so bad that we approached the Dagda, the king of the fairies, and explained our concerns. He agreed to meet us in Tír na n'Óg so that we could discuss what to do. But he tricked us. When all my brothers and I were in Tír na n'Óg he sealed the time skin and locked us in. We have a lot of power, Jenny, and we move freely between the worlds, but Tír na n'Óg is the Dagda's realm and he, too, has a great deal of power. As long as the time skin was sealed we couldn't cross through it. We were his prisoners.'

'So what happened?' said Jenny. 'How did you get out?'

'We agreed to bury the hatchet with the people of this world. Do you know what it means, to bury the hatchet?'

'I'm not sure,' said Jenny.

'It means to make peace,' said the púca. 'It means that both sides agree that hostilities are over. So while we were still locked in Tír na n'Óg, the people here found an old stone battle-axe, and when it was well and truly buried, and they had built that dirty great pile of rocks over it, the Dagda let us out.'

'The hatchet,' said Jenny. 'So that's what it's called. Not a chopper, a hatchet.'

'That's what it is,' said the púca. 'Just an old lump of rock, in fact. But it was the symbolism that mattered. The fairies might be tricksters but we are not. We are honour-bound to keep our word as long as the hatchet remains buried.'

JULY

1

On the twentieth of July, three days before JJ was due home, Aisling phoned the police again, and reported Jenny missing.

This time Jenny got home ten minutes after the guards arrived at the house, and this time they were a lot less sympathetic. They gave Aisling a severe lecture about the responsibilities of parenthood and the dangers lying in wait for children who were allowed too much freedom. Aisling took the opportunity to explain how difficult Jenny was, and how she never listened to either of her parents, and how their other children were all perfectly well balanced and dependable. The guards suggested she get in touch with social services if she was having problems; she couldn't keep wasting valuable Garda time like this.

Which was exactly what she had wanted them to say. Because next time she phoned them they would ignore her. And next time, in just a few short weeks, Jenny really would be gone.

For ever.

2

'So where does the ghost come in?' said Jenny.

She was sprawled with the púca in a mossy glade in the middle of the woods. Sunshine burst between the branches and the púca's white coat glowed so brightly that it almost hurt her eyes to look at him.

'He came in a long time later,' said the púca. 'It was after the war between the fairies and the ploddies, and—'

'Who?'

The púca laughed. 'The ploddies. That's what the fairies call the people of this world.'

'Ploddies,' said Jenny. She laughed. Somehow, although no one had ever told her so, she knew that she was not one of them.

'Anyway,' said the púca, 'the ploddies seem to have no loyalty for their gods, and sooner or later a new one was bound to come along. It caused a war between the fairies and the ploddies, and the fairies were banished to Tír na n'Óg and forbidden to set foot in this world again. So after that, with the fairies out of the way, we reopened negotiations about the state of this world. We had to. Things were going from bad to worse. There were no bears left in Ireland by then, and hardly any wolves. And this' – he gestured towards the mountain – 'had begun to happen.'

'What?' said Jenny.

'This . . . this desert. The Burren wasn't always like this, you know. All this endless bare rock. There were forests here once, and after that there was the best pastureland in the whole of Ireland. That was why too many people settled here and kept too much livestock, and why the soil became depleted and began to erode.'

'Wow,' said Jenny. 'I never knew that.'

'But we did, and what we saw broke our hearts,' said the púca. 'We asked the chieftain here to stop the destruction and move his people somewhere else. We said that if he didn't we would unearth the hatchet and return to open warfare. He wouldn't agree. So we went up the mountain to dig up the hatchet, but we found we had been tricked again. By the time we got there he had posted his son's ghost on guard, and he has been there ever since.'

Jenny, deep in thought, said nothing. The story was coming together at last, and something about it was making her uneasy.

'We are the gods of the material world, Jenny,' the púca went on. He reached out a hand and grabbed a fistful of soil and leaves from the woodland floor. 'This is our realm. The earth and the air, the leaves, the grasses, the birds and the beasts. We have no understanding of the spirit world and no jurisdiction over it. A human ghost is a very powerful thing. They cannot move themselves, but they can move other things. Small things. Like molecules in the brain, and in nerve endings.' He shuddered again. 'Very nasty, having your nerve endings twisted. It can do permanent damage, even to us. That's why one little ghost can hold us at bay for ever.'

'I see,' said Jenny quietly. She thought for a while, and then went on: 'So he isn't deluded after all? There *are* monsters. The monsters are you.'

The púca stretched his long, loose limbs and yawned. 'That's what he thinks, Jenny,' he said. 'But what do you think? Do I look like a monster to you?'

3

Jenny tried to explain to the ghost that there were no monsters. She told him that she had travelled far and wide and that she had never seen them. She told him that she had asked JJ, who had travelled to every continent in the world, and that he had never seen them either. But she was wasting her breath. The ghost was adamant in his beliefs and he was not about to be moved. He wanted to be free, she knew that. She could sense the longing in him. But he really seemed to believe that the fate of the human race was in his hands, and nothing she could say would change his mind.

She might have stopped visiting the ghost altogether if it hadn't been for the púca. He persuaded her to keep on going.

'He's so lonely and deluded,' he said to her. 'I hate to think of him being without a friend. It will take time, I know, but I'm sure that in the end you can persuade him to see the truth.'

But Jenny didn't think she could. She had become bored with the ghost; tired of his eulogies about the nobility of the human spirit and the general worthiness of mankind. He wasn't the fine, courageous soul she had first thought him, but a sad, mixed-up character, imprisoned by his own delusions. She viewed him, if not with contempt, then certainly with a degree of condescension. She found it hard to think of things to talk about, and since the ghost never saw anything new he was short of conversational openings. Sometimes, on a clear day, she quite enjoyed sitting in silence on top of the beacon and looking out over the plain and the sea beyond, but the truth was that she would rather have been with the púca, learning how to read the winds.

She came to understand many, many things from watching them. In school she had learned a bit about pollution and global warming, but the weather winds taught her to mistrust people who told children to recycle their pop bottles and turn off the tap when they brushed their teeth, but drove everywhere by car and flew off in aeroplanes several times a year for cheap weekend breaks. They taught her about the melting ice caps, the winds in perpetual fury, the droughts and the floods and the landslides. They brought her news of the death of the rainforests, the despair of the whales, and the extinction of deep-water fish species, vacuumed up from their lightless homes to explode on the decks of factory ships. She read of the relentless expansion of the human race into every dark and deep corner and every high, bright place on the surface of the earth. And, when she learned to read them, the winds of change taught her that all this would soon be coming to an end.

But what kind of an end, she didn't have the skill to understand.

AUGUST

1

One very early morning in late August Jenny got up and found JJ, Aisling and Donal already downstairs, apparently waiting for her. Aisling looked very unhappy. Her eyes were red, as though she had been crying all night, and Jenny wondered whether something terrible had happened while she was asleep. JJ looked bright and chirpy, but he kept smiling at her in a reassuring kind of way which made her feel anything but reassured. There was something up, Jenny was sure.

'We're going on a little adventure,' JJ said. 'You and me and Donal.'

Donal was yawning vigorously and didn't look at all enthusiastic.

'What kind of adventure?' said Jenny suspiciously.

'A magical mystery tour,' said JJ.

'Do we have to go in the car?' said Jenny, trying to think of an excuse to back out.

'Nope,' said JJ. 'We're walking.'

He bent to put on his boots and Donal, still yawning, started putting on his as well. Jenny waited for someone to tell her to put hers on, but nobody did, so she didn't.

Aisling was wearing a peculiar smile that looked as if it had been glued on top of an entirely different expression. It had, too. When she came to wave them off at the door she suddenly threw her arms around Jenny and burst into tears.

'Goodbye, sweetheart,' she said. 'Have a lovely time.'

JJ hustled the children out ahead of him and turned back to speak to Aisling.

'If we're not back in two days' time send Séadna Tobín to fetch us. But, whatever you do, don't let him bring his fiddle.'

Jenny knew Séadna Tobín. He was the pharmacist in Kinvara. His son ran the shop now, but Séadna was nearly always there, pottering around the place and chatting to the customers.

'Why Séadna Tobín?' asked Jenny as they set out along the track which ran up towards the top meadows of the farm. 'Where are we going?'

JJ's smile was now completely genuine and stretched from ear to ear. 'We're going to a really special place, Jen. It's a secret place and it's so nice that it's easy to forget to come back. The only other person round here who knows about it is Séadna.'

'What's the place called?' said Donal.

'It's called Tír na n'Óg,' said JJ. 'The land of eternal youth.'

'Don't be ridiculous,' said Donal. 'That's not a real place.'

'Want to bet?' said JJ.

He had thought long and hard about Donal and the best way of explaining everything to him. When he had told Hazel, her reactions had been mixed. Although she had agreed to go along with his plan he wasn't sure she really believed him. He didn't want Donal growing up with any doubts about Jenny's disappearance, so in the end he and Aisling had decided that he should go along and see for himself.

Jenny, on the other hand, did not need to be convinced about the existence of Tír na n'Óg. The púca had already told her all about it. She wasn't sure how she felt about going there, though. The sunshine and the dancing and everything sounded OK, but what if the Dagda sealed the time skin and she couldn't get out?

'Well, where is it, then?' Donal was saying. They had reached the end of the track and were walking through the gate into the top meadow, the one with the old ring fort in it.

'It's not far,' said JJ. 'You'll be amazed when you see how we get there.'

Donal was wearing a resentful expression, but his eyes suddenly widened and he pointed ahead, upwards and to the right. 'Look!'

JJ looked. The white goat was careering across the mountain slopes at an unbelievable speed. They watched its progress until it plunged into a hazel-filled hollow and vanished from sight.

'I wonder what's got into him,' said JJ, doing his best to hide his concern from the children.

Jenny was wondering, too. In all the time she had known the púca she had never seen him move at anything faster than a gentle trot.

They walked across the meadow, their footsteps making parallel tracks in the dew. They had taken a good crop of hay from it, and now a bright new growth was pushing through the cut stalks. This year they hadn't sold the hay, but had stored it in the barn. In a week or two JJ would put cattle in here to eat this new grass. And they would be his own cattle. He had already applied to the Department of Agriculture for a herd number. No more touring, he had promised Aisling. He would stay at home, farm his cattle, make his fiddles and help with the new baby.

If they had one. It all seemed totally unreal now, out here in the summer dawn.

'Are we going to the fort?' asked Donal.

'We are,' said JJ.

'Why?'

'Because the way into Tír na n'Óg is in there.'

'No it isn't,' said Donal, who was convinced this was all a stupid joke. 'I've been to the fort millions of times and I've never seen the entrance to Tír na n'Óg.'

'Ah,' said JJ, 'but have you been down the souterrain?'

'The what?'

'You didn't know about that, did you?'

'What's a souterrain?' said Jenny.

'It's an underground shelter. There are two chambers down there, under the fort.'

'Really?' said Donal. 'Like a bunker or something?'

'Just like a bunker,' said JJ, 'only very, very old.'

'How come I've never seen it?' said Donal. Jenny was surprised by this as well. She thought she knew every inch of this mountainside, and that included the fort.

'There are stones across the opening,' said JJ, but he didn't tell them about the wall that wasn't really a wall, but a barrier that kept time in this world and out of Tír na n'Óg. It was easier to show people things like that than to try and explain them.

They came to the rough circle of hawthorn trees and stepped over the encircling bank of grass and stones.

'So where is this underground thingy?' said Donal.

'It's just—' JJ stopped. They all did. Standing between them and the mouth of the souterrain was a big white goat.

And, this time, JJ had no doubt at all that he was a púca.

2

As they watched, the púca lengthened and straightened. He was still mostly goat, but he was man-shaped now. Jenny noticed that whenever he did this his knee and elbow joints changed direction. That was always the bit she liked the best. He sat down languidly on a rock. Jenny made to go towards him but JJ grabbed her by the collar.

'Let her come,' said the púca. 'If I intended to harm her I would have done it long before now.'

JJ let go of Jenny and she skipped over the lumpy ground and sat at the púca's feet. Donal, petrified, clutched at JJ's sleeve.

'Not a bad day,' said the púca, in a conversational tone.

JJ cleared his throat. 'Not bad at all,' he said.

'And where would you be going on such a fine day?' said the púca.

JJ shrugged. 'Oh,' he said, 'just strolling—'

'Tír na n'Óg,' said Jenny. 'Through the souterrain.'

'How interesting,' said the púca. 'Taking the fairy child home, were you, JJ?'

'Fairy child?' said Jenny.

'Um, well . . .' JJ stammered.

'But she's only half grown,' said the púca. 'You can't take a half-grown fairy child home, can you? Surely that can't be right?'

'Fairy child?' said Jenny again.

JJ was trying his best to think, but he wasn't having much success. Strictly speaking it was none of the púca's business what JJ did with Jenny, but he found himself extremely reluctant to tell him so. His eyes were yellow with black slits of pupils; more like a reptile's than a mammal's. And he remembered how the púca had grown and towered over him in Tír na n'Óg and how he had mesmerized him. He didn't want to do anything to get on the wrong side of him now.

'No,' he said finally. 'Maybe it isn't right. Not strictly. But Aengus didn't keep his side of the bargain, and I—'

A delighted laugh from the púca cut him short. 'Aengus Óg?' he said. 'You made an agreement with Aengus Óg and you expected him to stick to it?' He laughed again, as though he had never heard anything so hilarious in his life, and JJ struggled to swallow his irritation. Donal was still hanging on to his sleeve, peering out from behind him. It made him feel protective and it gave him courage.

'I don't see why that's so funny,' he said.

'It's funny because of all the feckless—'

The púca stopped, because JJ wasn't paying attention to him. He was looking at Jenny, who was staring at him with a bewildered expression. Her eyes were wide and there were tears glistening in them.

It cut JJ to the quick. Jenny hadn't cried since she was a baby. Not once, as far as he knew. This was never supposed to happen. It hadn't been part of the plan. Once Jenny saw Tír na n'Óg she would be so delighted to be home that she wouldn't mind at all about any kind of deal.

'Who's Aengus?' she said, in a quavering voice.

'You'll find out,' said JJ. 'As soon as the púca lets us through.'

But the púca had no intention of letting them go anywhere. 'What was the deal, JJ?' he said. 'What did he bribe you with?'

'It doesn't matter,' said JJ.

Suddenly, impossibly, the púca was looming over him, his huge lizard eyes numbing his will.

'It matters!' an enormous voice boomed between his ears.

Donal squealed and hauled on JJ's sleeve, but JJ

stood his ground. 'Wood,' he said, not entirely sure whether he had made the decision to tell, or whether the púca had made it for him. 'For making fiddles. Chiming maple.'

The púca was back to his normal size again, and sitting calmly on his rock.

'Chiming maple,' he said thoughtfully. 'Not a heavy price, I would have thought, in return for rearing a changeling. Cheap, if you ask me.'

JJ could feel Donal trembling violently behind him. Jenny, he noticed, had moved away from the púca and was staring at him, wide-eyed. JJ felt like a traitor.

'Keep her, JJ,' said the púca. 'She's not big enough to go home yet.'

'Fine, fine,' said JJ, thinking fast and trying to repair some of the damage he had inflicted upon Jenny. 'I wasn't going to leave her there anyway. I just wanted to put a bit of pressure on Aengus Óg.'

'Well,' said the púca lazily. 'We'll see if we can't sort you out a bit of timber, shall we?'

He leaned forward on the rock, became all goat again, and set off across the meadow towards the house. He moved rapidly, ignoring the farm track and heading in a straight line across the fields, jumping the stone walls as he went. JJ and the children began to follow, but they hadn't yet reached the gate of the top meadow when they saw something that stopped them in their tracks. The púca had come to an abrupt halt in the field called Molly's Place and was nosing around at the back of the farm buildings. Then he began to grow, swelling and stretching until he was as tall as the house, then taller still, towering over the spruce trees that lined the top end of the drive. He was so huge that they could see his yellow eyes from where they stood, and the bright, keen focus in them as he bent and plunged a gigantic fist straight into the solid ground.

The earth beneath their feet shook and they could feel, rather than hear, some monstrous subterranean rumble. Then, in an explosion of soil and rock, the púca's fist reappeared, and in it, like a bunch of twigs in a child's hand, was a whole tree. The púca heaved it clear of the earth then dropped it with a crash like a thunderclap, into the middle of Molly's Place. The tree bounced, its branches bending and snapping, then finally settled in a tremor of twigs and a gentle shower of huge red leaves. And, like a deflating balloon, the púca vanished behind it.

3

For a few moments the world was silent and still. The Burren hills basked in the fresh morning light. The dew began to lift. In the fort behind JJ and the children, a yellowhammer began to sing.

Donal took JJ's hand. They were both trembling.

'What happened?' said Donal.

'Um,' said JJ. 'It looks as if the púca just got me some wood. For my fiddles.'

'Where did he get it from?' said Donal.

JJ reached for Jenny's hand, but she was just a bit too far away and she was, as it seemed to him she always had been, occupying her own thoughts, her own space, her own private, separate little world. What he had done to her was still causing him pain.

'Jenny?' he said.

She didn't answer. There were a lot of things that she needed to think about, and the most important thing, at that moment, was what she had just seen. The púca had become bigger, that was all. But there was something about the size of him, and those huge, yellow eyes and curling horns, that she recognized. The ghost had seen this, too.

JJ and Donal set out across the meadow and, cautiously, Jenny followed. They joined the farm track and turned off it into Molly's Place. The tree was enormous, at least twenty metres long and nearly as wide. Its branches and its bare roots towered above their heads.

Aisling was standing beside it, with Aidan in her arms. He was uncharacteristically quiet, but pointed out the tree to JJ and the others as they arrived, in case they might have missed it. He hadn't been on the planet all that long, but it was long enough to know that a tree appearing out of nowhere was worth remarking upon.

'I assume this has something to do with you,' said Aisling.

JJ nodded. On the opposite side of the tree, just visible between its branches, the white goat was making a feast of the fresh red leaves. And as they watched, a young man stepped into view beside him. Only JJ recognized him, and only he knew how he had appeared, as if from nowhere.

'Are you responsible for this?' the man said to the goat.

The púca stood on his hind legs and became man-shaped. 'Just collecting a debt, Aengus Óg, since it was clear you weren't about to deliver it.'

'A debt?' said Aengus, his voice barely concealing his underlying rage. 'Since when have I owed you a tree?'

'Not me,' said the púca. He jerked a hairy thumb in JJ's direction, and Jenny wondered where it had come from. Goats, she was fairly certain, did not have thumbs.

Aengus walked around the crown of the tree until he could see the family. 'JJ Liddy!' he exclaimed. 'My God. How did you get so old?'

'The nerve of you!' said JJ. 'I'm only forty-two!' But he could not keep the smile from his face. Despite everything, he was delighted to see Aengus again.

'Is it you that wanted the tree?' said Aengus.

'Well, not a tree exactly. But you promised me some wood for making fiddles. Remember? That was the deal we made.'

Aengus looked uncertain.

'In return for bringing up your child,' JJ went on.

'Oh, yes,' said Aengus. 'That's right. But what's the rush? I was just getting around to it.' He was looking at Aidan, who was still in Aisling's arms.

'It's not that one,' said JJ. 'It's this one.'

He put a hand on Jenny's back and pressed her gently towards Aengus. 'Meet your father, Jenny,' he said.

Aengus stared at her. 'It can't be,' he said. 'How did she get that big already?'

'The same way I got so old,' said JJ. 'It's been eleven years, Aengus.'

'Eleven years,' said Aengus. 'Well, well.' He beamed a smile at Jenny, full of charm and self-confidence. 'It's wonderful to meet you.'

But Jenny had already had more than enough for one day. Ignoring Aengus, she threw a furious look at JJ then turned and ran towards the back yard of the house.

'Wait!' Aengus called after her. 'There's something I want to tell you!'

Jenny stopped and turned back to look at him.

'If there's anything you need, just call me. I mean it. Just shout. I'll hear you.'

Jenny didn't answer. She went into the yard and disappeared from sight.

'Well,' said Aengus. 'Children these days, eh?'

'She's just a bit overwhelmed, I imagine,' said Aisling, and JJ realized he hadn't introduced them.

'My wife, Aisling,' he said. 'And this is Aidan, and my other son, Donal. This is Aengus, Donal. He's . . . er . . . your great-grandfather.'

Donal was also just a bit overwhelmed, and he decided to ignore Aengus's outstretched hand and follow Jenny back to the house.

184

'Donal plays the box,' said JJ, as though that explained his reticence.

Aengus nodded. 'Nice children,' he said. Then his beautiful features clouded over again and he turned back to the púca.

'And tell me this,' he said tersely. 'What does this puck goat have to do with anything?'

'Just helping out,' said the púca, and butter wouldn't melt in his mouth.

'Just sticking your hairy snout into things that don't concern you,' said Aengus. 'There's a reason for that, I dare say, but I don't suppose you're about to share it with us. The cloven-footed races are not famous for their neighbourly gestures.'

He stared at the púca and the púca stared back.

Aengus went on: 'Might I suggest that you shove off and stop meddling in other people's affairs?' He tore a few leaves off the tree and tossed them at the púca. 'Here. Take your picnic with you.'

The púca began to swell and JJ stepped back and took Aisling's hand. But the violence that he had feared did not materialize. Instead, the púca became a goat again and began to wander nonchalantly away across the meadow.

'Don't trust him, JJ,' said Aengus. 'A charming fellow, no doubt, but a member of the devil class.'

'I don't know who to trust,' said JJ. 'At least he came up with the goods.'

Aengus's green eyes flashed dangerously and JJ realized he was pushing his luck.

'I'm sorry about the tree,' he went on. 'It wasn't my idea. All I wanted was enough wood for a few fiddles.'

'No bother,' said Aengus. 'Keep it. Make a couple of cellos. Turn the off-cuts into candlesticks. I tell you what. Make a fiddle for me while you're at it. You can send it with little Whatsername when she's ready to come home.'

'Hardly,' said JJ. 'That wood will need to be seasoned for at least eight years before I can start using it, and Jenny will be back in Tír na n'Óg well before then.'

'No worries,' said Aengus. 'Bring it yourself whenever it's made. I'll be there.'

'You will,' said JJ, 'but I'm not so sure about me. Do you realize I'll be fifty before I can start using that wood?'

'That's always the way with ploddies,' said Aengus. 'They don't last. But, listen, if it ever starts getting scary just come on over to Tír na n'Óg and stay with us. You'd be welcome. We'd be delighted to have you.'

And with that, Aengus waved to Aisling and Donal, walked around to the other side of the tree, and vanished into thin air.

4

'I suppose this means that it's all off, then,' said Aisling. 'With Jenny and the baby and everything.'

'I'd say so,' said JJ. 'Maybe it's the best outcome in the end. You should have seen poor Jenny's face when she figured out what was up.'

Asling nodded. 'I'm glad she's back, even though she's a pain in the neck sometimes. I was in bits here when you were gone, thinking I'd never see her again.'

'Hmm,' said JJ. 'It was all a bit hasty all right.'

'So we'd better call Hazel back,' said Aisling. 'Tell her it's all off, about the baby and everything.'

'Yep,' said JJ. 'Get the whole family back together again and get on with our lives. And I'd better start by doing a bit of explaining.'

He wanted to speak to Jenny and Donal together, but when he got inside he found that Jenny had shut herself in her room. When he knocked she told him to go away. She was traumatized, he knew, and he wasn't surprised. He remembered how disorientated he had been when he got back from Tír na n'Óg, and in some ways what she and Donal had been through was worse. The púca, the tree and the sudden appearance of Aengus Óg had all broken the rules of nature as they understood them, and it would take time for them to come to terms with it all. And for Jenny it was worse again, because she had also discovered that she was adopted; not a Liddy at all but a fairy changeling; not a citizen of Kinvara but a visitor, passing through.

He left her to work things out on her own for a while, and went down to find Donal. He was in the sitting room watching the television, but he appeared to have forgotten to turn it on.

'We'd better make a start on that tree,' JJ said to him. 'In case someone comes along and wonders how it got there.'

While they were in the shed oiling the chainsaw and setting the blade and hunting for petrol and goggles and gloves, JJ told Donal about Anne Korff, the publisher who had shown him how to get to Tír na n'Óg through the souterrain, and about how amazed he had been when he first went through the wall. While they were walking out to Molly's Place together he told him about the time leak, which was the reason he had gone to Tír na n'Óg, and about how he and Aengus had discovered the priest who was causing it, and how he had fooled him into stopping it.

For a long time after that they said nothing, because JJ was busy with the chainsaw, lopping off the smaller branches, and it made a lot of noise. But when he turned it off and they were gathering the twiggy bits and piling them up for burning, he told Donal about the injured dog, Bran, and how he had brought her back with him when he returned.

'There was nothing left of her, though,' he said. 'Just a handful of dust. And that's where the danger lies, when you go to Tír na n'Óg. Because there's no time there, there's no way of knowing how much of it is passing over here. The fairy folk can come and go as they please, but we can't. If you don't come back within the time of your own natural life-span, it's just too bad.'

'Is that why you told Mum to send Séadna Tobín in after us?' said Donal.

'That's exactly why,' said JJ.

'And what happened to the priest?'

'Father Doherty?' said JJ. 'I'm afraid the same thing happened to him as happened to Bran. He came through the time wall and there was nothing left of his life on this side. They found his bones in the souterrain.'

'My God,' said Donal. 'That's creepy. And what about Anne Korff? What happened to her?'

189

'She's still there,' said JJ. 'She must have decided not to come back.' He thought about her, and realized that when he saw her next, she would look exactly as she had done when he last saw her a quarter of a century ago.

'And could she come back now?' said Donal. 'If she wanted to?'

JJ thought about it. 'She probably could, yes,' he said. 'But she would be very old.'

'The same age she would be if she had stayed here and never gone to Tír na n'Óg?'

'Exactly,' said JJ. 'You've got it.'

He picked up the chainsaw again and went back to the tree.

Later on that day, JJ succeeded in getting Jenny to talk to him. He went over many of the same things he had told Donal, and a few more as well. He told her about her mother, Drowsy Maggie, and about what fun it was in Tír na n'Óg, and how no one ever had any worries about money or health or responsibility.

'So why did I have to come here at all?' said Jenny. 'Why couldn't I just stay there with my parents?'

'Because there's no time there. Nothing changes. If you had stayed there you wouldn't have grown up. You'd still be a baby, like our baby is.'

'Your baby?'

'We swapped you. Our baby is still there, still in Tír na n'Óg. When you go back there – when you decide the time is right – we'll bring her back home with us.'

Jenny wished she hadn't heard about this. It was one thing too many. She had never been afraid before, but now she was. She felt raw, as though her skin was inside out, and every unexpected noise made her jump. She also felt very small and very much alone. She hadn't known what trust was until she lost it. She missed her parents, even though they were still there, because they weren't her parents any more. They were someone else. All those people that she had taken for granted were not what they had seemed. They were distant figures with their own plans and purposes, and she meant nothing to them. For the first time she had an insight into what Aisling and JJ and Hazel had meant when they talked about their feelings, and how other people could hurt them.

But the one who had hurt Jenny the most had been the púca. She had trusted him absolutely. She had believed that the ghost was deluded because he had told her so. She had believed that there weren't any monsters. With her new, inside-out skin she could imagine how it felt to be the boy ghost, standing alone on the top of the beacon on the top of the mountain and defending it single-handedly. She wished she could go to him and tell him what had happened; tell him she believed, after all, that he was right. But she knew the púca wouldn't let her. She understood, now, what part she had played in JJ's plans. And she was beginning to get an inkling of why it was that the púca had shown so much interest in her.

She looked up. JJ was waiting for a response from her. She searched for something suitable.

'I always knew I was different,' she said finally. 'And now I know why.'

'There's nothing wrong with being different, Jen,' said JJ. 'Myself and Aisling think the world of you, please believe that.'

But even as he said it, JJ knew how hollow those words must sound. He reached out and gave Jenny a hug, but he learned nothing from that. She had always been a distant and unresponsive child, and she was no different now.

5

Even with Donal's tireless help, it took JJ the best part of two days to cut up the tree and clear away the debris. He hated every minute of the work. He remembered standing under a tree like that in Tír na n'Óg, and hearing it resonate and ring with harmonies when he blew a note on his great-grandfather's flute. It was possibly the very same one. Cutting it up now felt like butchery. The gradual wilting of those beautiful red leaves was the worst part, and made him wonder whether the greatest instruments in the world would be worth the death of this glorious fairy tree.

On the third day he borrowed a strong trailer from Peter Hayes and hitched it up to the car. He had cut the trunk of the chiming maple into three pieces, and he used the front-loader of his old tractor to get them on to the trailer. Then, at four o'clock in the morning of the fourth day, he set out for Waterford.

It was a long drive, but well worth it. There was a

sawmill there run by a man who specialized in cutting timber for fine furniture and instrument making, and JJ was taking no chances with this tree. He drove slowly and it took him nearly five hours to get there, which gave him plenty of time for thinking. He spent most of it dreaming of what Aengus had said to him about going to stay in Tír na n'Óg. The sense of timelessness there had been so blissful, and the company of those easy-going people so pleasant. There were fewer time constraints in everyone's lives now that the leak had been stopped, but there were still plenty of other pressures and responsibilities that he would love to escape. He had never gone back before now because he had been afraid of getting it wrong, and letting his earthly life pass by while he was playing the fiddle and dancing.

But the idea of retiring there was a new one, and very attractive. He would have to wait until the children grew up of course, but, after that, what was there to stop him? Aisling could come too, if she wanted to. It would be hard to move her piano, but she could learn to play something else instead. And when the children had passed the best of their lives in this world, what was to stop them coming over as well? He envisaged generation upon generation of middle-aged Liddys basking in the perpetual sunshine of Tír na n'Óg, immune to the passage of time in this world; the place that the fairies called the land of the dying.

6

While JJ's wood was being sawn in Waterford there was a surprise visitor at the Liddy house. He didn't knock, but walked in through the back door and lowered himself, with great difficulty, into the armchair beside the range. Aidan discovered him there, during one of his armed patrols of the house, and the visitor sent him to fetch Donal.

'Quick,' said Mikey, when Donal came in. 'I forgot my glasses. What time does that say?'

He held out his arm and Donal read the time on his wristwatch.

'It says quarter to ten,' said Donal, 'but it's wrong. It's about two hours slow.'

'Never mind the hours,' said Mikey. 'I'm only looking at the big hand. I'd say I've been here five minutes now, which means it took me just over half an hour to get here. Not bad for an old man, wouldn't you say?'

'Did you walk over?' said Donal, putting on the kettle.

'I did,' said Mikey. 'How else would I ever get to hear a tune these days?'

Donal blushed. 'I'm sorry I haven't been over lately,' he said.

'Ah, don't mind that!' said Mikey. 'I'm only winding you up. But I said it's time I got into training so I've made a start. I walked round the whole of the home farm yesterday and I'm up as far as here today.'

'Training for what?' said Donal.

'The Dublin City Marathon,' said Mikey. 'I start running tomorrow.'

Jenny came in at that point and Mikey turned to her. 'Did you hear that, girleen? I'm going running the marathon.'

Jenny didn't know what the marathon was, so the joke was lost on her.

'You're not really going running tomorrow, are you, Mikey?' said Donal.

'Maybe not tomorrow.' The humour left Mikey's face abruptly. 'Maybe we'll get up to the top of the mountain first. God knows, I'll have no peace until I do.'

'The trouble is,' said Donal, 'I'm afraid we couldn't get the helicopter. Dad . . . we tried all the helicopter companies in the phone book but they only do golf tours.'

'Golf tours,' said Mikey flatly. 'There's a thing. But thank your father for trying, anyway. I had an idea it wasn't going to work in any case.'

Aisling came into the kitchen and was astonished to see Mikey installed in the chair.

'How did you get here, Mikey?' she said.

'I walked,' said Mikey. 'Every step of the way.'

Aisling was instantly filled with guilt. Mikey had been a saviour during the time when Hazel was small and JJ was away at college. She was a 'blow-in' and didn't know many people in the area. There had been a few good neighbours, but Mikey was the best. He called over nearly every day on his way up the mountainside to look at the cattle, always ready to stop and chat, always patient and entertaining with Hazel. If Aisling was depressed he cheered her up, and if she was feeling cynical he restored her faith in human nature. When he had given up the winterage at the top of the farm, unable to make the long climb any more, he had still walked over as far as the house, just to pay her a visit. She regretted that she didn't find more time to return those visits, now that he found it so difficult to get around.

She took over the making of the tea. A minute or two later Aidan came in and stood surveying Mikey, as though wondering how to get rid of him.

'Is Belle outside?' said Donal. 'Can I give her a biscuit?'

'She's at home in the house,' said Mikey. 'She must be the stupidest dog ever walked the earth, that one. I can't get anywhere when she comes with me. You'd swear she was doing her best to make me fall.'

'Poor Belle,' said Donal. 'I don't think she's stupid. I think she just likes being close to you.'

'Close is one thing,' said Mikey. 'Under my feet is another.'

'Go home,' said Aidan.

'I'll go home when I'm good and ready,' said Mikey. 'And you mind your manners.'

Jenny got bored and began a new, aimless circuit of the house. She hadn't been outside since the day the tree arrived, and now that she was spending more time inside she was discovering things that she had never noticed before. The pile of unused instrument cases in the corner of the sitting room had a spider city built behind it. The window in Donal and Aidan's bedroom didn't close properly. And the front door, which had always seemed so heavy and solid when she was trying to sneak out through it, was a flimsy defence. One tap on it from the púca and all those glass panels would shatter into tiny pieces. Jenny knew she wasn't safe anywhere.

She couldn't decide whether she preferred being on her own or with the others, so she went back into the kitchen to find out. Aisling had poured the tea. Mikey was drinking his rapidly, with an interesting variety of noises.

'Will I get the accordion and play you a tune?' said Donal.

'I don't think so,' said Mikey. 'Not this time. If I sit here much longer I'll seize up entirely and you'll have to get a crane to lift me out.'

Mikey handed his cup to Aisling, and Aidan took the opportunity to dash in and give him an open-handed smack on the knee. With surprising speed, Mikey grabbed his hand before he could pull it free.

'Good man,' he said to Aidan. 'Give me a hand up, now.'

'Noo,' Aidan wailed, trying to pull his hand away. Mikey used his struggling and pulling to get up out of the chair. Or, at least, he pretended to.

'By God, you're strong for a young fella,' he said, letting go of his hand at last.

Aidan stood in the centre of the room, torn between flight and flattery.

'Will you be all right, Mikey?' said Aisling. 'I can't give you a lift because JJ's got the car.'

'I'll be fine,' said Mikey. 'Why wouldn't I?'

'Shall I come with you?' said Donal.

'No,' said Mikey. 'But d'you know what you'll do? Go up into the hazel woods there this afternoon and cut me a good long stick' – he joined the tips of his thumb and forefinger to make a circle – 'about this thick' – then held his hand, palm down, level with his shoulder – 'and that long. It'll be a great help to me in my training.'

He stepped out into the sunshine and closed the door behind him.

Donal looked at Jenny. 'Will you come with me?'

Jenny shook her head.

'Yes you will,' said Aisling. 'We've all been cooped up in this house too long. We'll all go to the woods and get a stick for Mikey, and we'll bring Sergeant Aidan for the walk.'

7

John Duffy at the sawmill dropped everything to get JJ's wood sawn, so that he could get back on the road again. He was very impressed by the wood, and so was JJ when he saw it coming off the mill. It was beautifully figured, with the strong 'flame' and 'curl' so prized by instrument makers. John Duffy offered to buy some of it from him, to sell on to other customers, but JJ said he wouldn't sell at any price.

He asked John to cut the wood in different ways. He wanted mainly fiddle backs, but he asked for a few cello backs as well. Most of the wood was cut on the quarter, like very thin, very deep slices of a pie. This would make the flame show as horizontal stripes running across the backs of the instruments when they were made. Under the varnish, the stripes would appear to have three dimensions when they were moved around under the light. It was a sort of natural holographic effect, and was only to be found in the best of curly maple. It was the most common way for wood to be cut, but JJ asked for some to be slab-cut as well, which would give the fiddle backs a different, more irregular and unusual pattern.

When it was all cut and loaded back on the trailer, JJ set off again, and he had as much time for thinking on his way back as he'd had on his way there. More time than was healthy, perhaps, because it was during that long drive that he came up with an extraordinary idea. He tried very hard to dismiss it, but once it had appeared he just couldn't get rid of it. It was meeting the púca that had given rise to the seed of the idea. Or meeting the púca again, because he was as sure as he could be that he was the same one he had met in Tír na n'Óg. It had made him think back to that earlier meeting, and he had remembered something the púca had said:

'Do you want to know the real magic that is at work in the world?' And there had been something else: 'Do you know who we are, who walk between the worlds and haunt the wild places of the earth?'

What worlds? That was what JJ wanted to know. Just this one and Tír na n'Óg, or were there others? In his mind was a fixed memory of his grandfather's flute when he had first taken it out of the wall between this world and Tír na n'Óg. One end of it, the Tír na n'Óg end, was clean and shiny. The other end, which had been exposed to the passage of time, was dusty and covered with cobwebs, and noticeably darker in colour. One end, in effect, was older than the other.

JJ tried again to put the idea out of his mind and forget about it. He just couldn't.

When he arrived home it was late, and he was exhausted. He had a quick cup of tea and a bite to eat, then enlisted Donal and Jenny to help him unload the sawn timber. He had brought every last scrap of it home on the trailer, even the useless off-cuts, just in case John Duffy had been tempted to make a closer examination of it. He doubted anything would show up in analysis, but he didn't want to take any chances.

As he took it off the trailer, JJ separated the pieces into three piles. Donal took everything on the first pile into the loft of the cow byre and stacked it there. Jenny took the pieces from the second pile into the workshop, where she left them on the floor for JJ to stack later. The third pile was smaller, and was made up of some of the nicest pieces on the trailer. By the time he had finished unloading there was enough wood on that pile for the backs and matching necks of ten fiddles. About half of them were wedges for two-piece backs, tied with string into matching pairs. The rest were wider pieces for one-piece backs, and two of them were slab-cut. These last ones were JJ's favourites, and his fingers itched to start carving them into shape. They might have to keep itching for another eight years, but JJ had set aside that little pile for a particular reason. If his plan worked, he might be turning them into fiddles much, much sooner than that.

8

When they eventually climbed into bed that night Aisling told JJ about the trip to the woods to cut a stick for Mikey.

'Did you see the púca?' said JJ.

'No, no sign of him. But I'm very worried about Jenny.'

'Why?' said JJ.

'She's totally lost her confidence. She spent the whole trip hanging on to me as if her life depended on it. I've never seen her like that before.'

'She'll get over it,' said JJ. 'She's just had a few shocks, that's all. You didn't see the púca when it tore up that tree. It was pretty scary, you know.'

'Perhaps that's all it is,' said Aisling. 'But she must be feeling a bit insecure, knowing she's not our real daughter and all that.'

'I don't see what we can do about it, do you?' said JJ. 'Other than what we're doing?'

'No, I don't,' said Aisling, 'but I wish I did.'

She turned over and before long she was snoring softly. But, tired as he was, there was to be no sleep for JJ that night. He lay awake, staring into the darkness of the room, listening to the night calls of vixens and owls, and going over and over his plans for the following morning. He knew it was going to be dangerous and he was deeply afraid, but no matter how hard he tried he couldn't talk himself out of his decision.

At first light he got up quietly and went downstairs. He wasn't hungry but breakfast was an excuse for delaying his departure, so he made tea and toast and sat at the kitchen table until they were finished. Jenny, who still woke early even though she no longer went out, came down as he was getting up to leave. She didn't show any interest in where he was going, and he didn't invite her to come.

The previous evening he had packed all his specially selected wood into the biggest rucksack he had. It was alarmingly heavy and he was afraid that the bag wouldn't stand the strain, but he was reluctant to leave any of the wood behind. If his plan worked it might be the only chance he got, so he had to take all he could carry.

The straps cut into his shoulders as he walked across

the farmland, and the sharp corners of the slabs and wedges dug into his back. Despite his discomfort and the anxiety that dogged his every step, he found himself appreciating the fresh morning air and the energy of the birds as they soared and sang in the sunlight.

He scanned the hillside ahead of him. At first he couldn't see what he was looking for and he wondered if, today of all days, the púca would decide not to show. But eventually he spotted him, high, high up and far to his right, a little white dot perched on a rock at the very edge of the mountain top.

He stopped and adjusted the straps of the rucksack. It looked as though he had a long, arduous climb ahead of him, but if that was what it took he was prepared to undertake it. On the off-chance, though, he waved his hand in the púca's direction, three times in the biggest arc his arm could make. For a moment nothing happened. Then the púca began to descend and cross the hillside towards him.

JJ's heart stopped as his nerve failed. Was he really going to do this? It wasn't too late to change his mind and pull out. Then he remembered why he was doing it. His pulse restarted, racing at his throat, and his feet began to move again. He was going to make some of the best violins the world had ever seen.

No one could understand why the instruments made by the famous Antonius Stradivarius were so good. The most faithfully executed copies could not compare with the originals, even though all the dimensions were the same, right down to the last 0.1 of a millimetre. The fiddle that JJ played was an original 'Strad', although he didn't make this generally known. It had been a gift from the maker to Aengus Óg, who had left it behind him on one of his visits to JJ's grandmother, and it had been handed down in the family ever since.

Aengus had never asked for it back, but it was he who had told JJ that Stradivarius had made the backs of his violins from chiming maple. It had grown once on the ploddy side of the time skin, but every last tree had been cut down during the Middle Ages. Somehow Stradivarius had discovered the wood in Tír na n'Óg and had succeeded in acquiring regular supplies of it. Only JJ knew this, and he had every intention of exploiting his knowledge.

He crossed the wall at the top of the farm and continued to walk diagonally across the hillside in the direction of the púca. He was hidden from his sight now, by the crags and hollows which lay between them. There was a possibility, of course, that they wouldn't meet at all, but JJ thought it unlikely. There was no doubt that the púca had seen him.

At the edge of the hazel woods he stopped. His heart

was pounding, partly from the exertion of the climb and partly from a growing feeling of terror. He began to wonder what kind of madness was compelling him to do this. What was it that Aengus had said about púcas? 'Members of the devil class', that was it. But then Aengus himself was hardly the most reliable person he had ever met, and there was clearly some deeply held enmity between him and the púca. In Tír na n'Óg they had bad-mouthed each other. And the evidence from this world was that the púca was quite benign. Admittedly he had frightened the wits out of JJ and the children, but on the other hand he had been given plenty of opportunity to do harm, particularly to Jenny, and he never had.

Even so, that first step forward into the green shadows of the woods cost JJ every ounce of courage that he had. After a few paces he stopped again, letting his eyes adjust to the difference in the light and wishing his frantic pulse would settle. He took a few steadying breaths and moved on into the heart of the woods.

He didn't have to go far. The púca was waiting for him, in his long shape, sitting on a mossy rock and leaning against the silvery trunk of an ash tree.

'Hello, JJ,' he said.

JJ chose a rock for himself at a respectful distance and shrugged the heavy pack from his shoulders. It dropped with a rattle to the ground.

'Hello,' he said, trying to sound cheerful. 'Beautiful morning!'

'Ah, but isn't every morning beautiful, JJ? Isn't this whole world just the bee's knees?' The púca stretched languidly and crossed his legs. His hands, JJ noticed, had fingers and thumbs like his own, but his feet still had cloven hooves. 'But what has you up and about so early?'

JJ would have preferred to have beaten about the bush for a bit longer, but since the púca had asked he came straight out with it.

'I was looking for you, actually.'

'How exciting,' said the púca. 'It's very unusual these days for anybody to come looking for me. What can I do for you?'

'Well,' said JJ, 'I wanted to ask you something. You told me once that you walked between the worlds, and I was sort of wondering about whether that just meant, you know, between here and Tír na n'Óg, or whether there were other worlds as well.'

'There are indeed,' said the púca. 'More than you could count. But was there some particular kind of world you were looking for?'

JJ nodded. 'You know the way there's no time in Tír na n'Óg but there's time here, and it goes by at a certain speed? Well, I was wondering whether there might be a world where time goes by even faster than it does here.'

The púca laughed. 'Since you sat down on that rock,' he said, 'whole worlds have been born, lived out their existence and died again. Is that fast enough for you?'

'Whoa,' said JJ. 'That's a bit too fast.'

'But why would you want such a world?' said the púca. 'Are you tired of your existence? Are you in a big rush to spend the rest of your years?'

'No, no,' said JJ. 'It's not for me. I don't want to go there. I just want to send something there.' He reached into the rucksack and took out a quarter-sawn slab. 'I have this beautiful wood, you see, from the tree you got for me. But it's too fresh and I can't use it. It needs to cure for eight or ten years before I can make fiddles out of it.'

'I see,' said the púca. 'So the world is in a great rush for more fiddles, is it?'

'Well, not exactly,' said JJ. 'There are plenty of fiddles around. But these would be better.'

'And you need a better fiddle than you have?'

'Not me,' said JJ. 'I have a good one already. But I could sell them, you see.'

'They would be worth a lot of money, I imagine,' said the púca. He appeared to be battling with some kind of strong emotion, and JJ tensed. But the battle,

211

whatever it was, resulted in a smile. 'And you would become world famous as a violin-maker.'

'That's about the size of it, I suppose,' said JJ.

'I see,' said the púca. 'And for this you are willing to sell your soul?'

JJ's jaw dropped and the púca laughed. 'What you desire can be done, JJ. But do you think I'm just here to grant your wishes? Like a fairy godmother?'

'Well, no,' said JJ, although the bitter truth was that he had thought just that.

'No,' said the púca. 'I think I'll probably let you keep your soul. But if I age the wood for you, I will expect something in return.'

'Like what?' said JJ, suddenly far less keen on the whole idea.

'What would you think was fair?' said the púca. 'A pound of flesh, perhaps? A few pints of blood? The fingers of your left hand?'

JJ returned the slab to his rucksack. 'I'm not sure this was such a good plan after all,' he said.

'How typical of your race,' said the púca scathingly. 'You want everything and you want it now, but you know the true cost of nothing. Without so much as a second thought you strip the planet of its trees and drain it of its oil, and smother its skin with concrete.'

JJ's hackles rose. He knew that the planet was in serious danger, and at home he and the family lived as simple a life as any family he knew. But he felt extremely guilty about the number of aircraft flights he had been taking. 'Actually there are plenty of people with second thoughts,' he said. 'They're just not the same people who had the first thoughts.'

The púca, with a visible effort, reined himself in. 'Perhaps I'm not being fair,' he said. 'After all, you only want to make a few fiddles. It's a harmless enough occupation, isn't it? It's hardly heavy industry.'

JJ shook his head. 'It's so I can stay at home and do a bit of farming instead of flying around the world playing concerts. I would be doing the environment a favour.'

'Let's make a deal, then,' said the púca. 'There is, in fact, something I want, and it won't cost you an arm and a leg. I'm afraid I gave the little fairy child a fright when I fetched your tree for you the other day. She hasn't been to see me since then. It's so rare for me to have a friend and I miss her dreadfully. If I do this thing for you, will you promise to bring Jenny up here to see me, and help me to win back her confidence?'

JJ thought long and hard, but he couldn't find any objections. In all the time Jenny had been roaming the hillsides with the púca no harm had ever come to her. The main problems would arise when term started again.

'All right,' said JJ. 'But there's one condition. You mustn't let her take time out of school.'

'School?' said the púca. 'What use is schooling to a fairy child?'

'Not much, I agree,' said JJ. 'But if she doesn't go it creates big problems for my wife and me. The authorities, you know? They don't understand about púcas and fairies and all that stuff.'

'Hmm,' said the púca.

'She can come any time outside school hours,' JJ went on, 'but she can't keep taking time off.'

'You drive a hard bargain,' said the púca.

'Well . . .' said JJ. 'Maybe she could take one day a week off without too much hassle. But definitely no more than that.'

'Done,' said the púca abruptly. 'You have yourself a deal.'

Delighted with himself, JJ unpacked the wood. The púca stretched out a hand that was enormous, and way out of proportion to the rest of his body, but JJ was too excited to be shocked. He stacked the slabs, the wedges and the neck blocks in the massive palm, and when they were all there the púca closed his hairy fingers around them. He sat quite still for a moment, concentrating hard. Then, with terrifying speed and violence, he swung his arm up and punched a hole through some invisible membrane in the air. Fragments of brilliant green light splintered around his fist for an instant, and then it was gone. The púca's arm appeared to end at the wrist.

'How old do you need it to be?' he asked.

'About ten years?' said JJ. 'Twelve would be perfect.'

The púca nodded thoughtfully, waited a moment or two longer and then, in another scatter of flinty green splinters, withdrew his hand. It was absolutely filthy, covered with layers of grime and powdery, reddish dust. He dropped the pile of wood at JJ's feet and JJ inspected the top piece. It was just right; dry and hard and absolutely ready to be used.

The púca's hand had returned to its previous size and he was busy trying to brush the dirt off it with the other one.

'This is perfect,' said JJ. 'Thanks a million.'

'You're welcome,' said the púca, who was now wiping the dirty hand on the thick moss which covered a nearby rock. 'Just don't forget your side of the bargain, all right?'

'I won't,' said JJ, packing the wood back into the rucksack. 'I'll be back with Jenny before the day is out.'

9

Jenny was still the only one up when he got back, so he decided to take her up to see the púca straight away. He didn't even take off his boots, but dropped the rucksack in the workshop and went into the kitchen to collect her.

'Want to come and visit the púca?' he said.

'No,' said Jenny.

'Thing is,' said JJ, 'he's very upset about what happened the other day. He said he didn't mean to frighten you, and that he's very sorry and he misses you terribly.'

'Tough,' said Jenny firmly.

She hadn't forgotten that the last time she went somewhere with JJ it turned out that he was trying to get rid of her, and although she was, secretly, quite interested in going to Tír na n'Óg, she intended to do it when she was good and ready, and not before. Besides that she was frightened of the púca and harboured deep suspicions about his intentions. She had become convinced that she was as much a pawn in his game as she was in JJ's and she was determined to go nowhere near him.

JJ decided that, for once, honesty was the best policy. 'The thing is,' he said, 'I kind of promised that I would take you to see him. He did something for me, you see, and we made a deal.'

'What did he do for you?'

JJ took her into the workshop and showed her a piece of the unseasoned timber and a piece that the púca had aged for him.

'He made it older?' said Jenny. 'How?'

JJ explained about the different worlds, and the big fist, and the splinters of green light, and the grime and the red dust.

'Cool,' said Jenny. 'Amazing what he can do, isn't it?'

'Amazing,' said JJ. 'And he was so nice about it as well. So will you come with me to see him?'

'Nope,' said Jenny. 'No way.'

The first thing Donal thought about when he woke up was the púca and the tree, because something as dramatic and frightening as that took a long time to work its way to the back of a person's mind. The second thing he thought about was Mikey's stick.

He and Jenny and Aisling, and even Aidan, had all

cut sticks for themselves in the woods, but Donal had reserved the best one for Mikey. It was beautifully straight, with no bend or taper at all, and the only bulge in its entire length fell, Donal was certain, just below where Mikey's hand would be, and would make it easier for him to grip. It was light but strong and it was, Donal thought, just a little bit magic. It was a hazel rod for Mikey, to make him young and strong again.

When he got downstairs he found Jenny in the armchair, reading to Aidan. JJ was in the workshop, sorting and stacking timber and doing a general tidy up in there. He was in a cantankerous mood and it was all very noisy, so Donal ate his breakfast as quickly as he could, eager to get out of the house. And, to his surprise, Jenny was of like mind. As soon as she heard where he was going she deposited Aidan on the floor and got ready to go with him.

Jenny doubted that the púca was confined to the mountainside behind the house, but she had never seen him descend to the plain. There was a chance, she knew, that he would see them and come looking for her, but it was a risk worth taking. She was slowly going crazy, cooped up in the house all day, and she longed for the fresh air and the feel of the morning dew beneath her feet.

Donal had his own stick with him as well as Mikey's,

and he swung them alternately as he walked, using them like ski poles. Jenny had hers, too, and planted it firmly on the ground at every step. It made her feel strong and safe.

As they crossed Mikey's fields, Jenny spotted his blue-checked shirt in amongst the bushes of the old fort, so they changed direction and went to meet him there. They couldn't see anyone else, but as they drew closer they could hear that Mikey was talking to someone in there, and Donal remembered that this had happened once before.

They stopped and listened.

'Any day now,' Mikey was saying. 'Some day very soon. It might take a bit of time but I'll get up there. Either that or die trying.'

He went quiet for a while, as though expecting a reply, but neither Donal nor Jenny could hear one.

'Ah, I will,' Mikey went on. 'Bit by bit. Step by step. One foot in front of the other. Have no fear of it.' He paused again. 'I won't fall. Why should I? I'll take my time. And the Liddy boy is cutting a stick for me. That'll be a great help. I don't know why I didn't think of that a long time ago.'

At that point Donal and Jenny stepped into the fort and pushed through the bushes. They looked around, but there was no one else in there.

'There you are,' said Mikey. 'With my stick as well. Good man yourself.'

'Who were you talking to?' said Donal.

'The dog,' said Mikey. 'Because I do get tired of talking to myself.'

Belle was greeting them now, wagging her tail with delight.

'Were you talking about going up to the beacon?' said Donal.

'I was,' said Mikey. 'Did you hear me?'

'I don't think you should do it, Mikey,' said Donal. 'I think it's too dangerous.'

Mikey grinned mischievously. 'That's exactly what she said, but I soon set her straight. She won't be coming anyway, the way she gets under my feet, so it's none of her business what I do, and it's none of yours either, Donal Liddy. I'm old enough to make up my own mind, and that's exactly what I'll do.'

10

It had never occurred to JJ that Jenny might refuse to go with him and he was worried about the consequences. There had been no mention of what might happen if he didn't keep his end of the bargain and now he wished he'd thought of adding some sort of get-out clause to the contract.

He pottered around the workshop for a while, trying to come up with a solution, but in the end he realized that there was no alternative to facing the music. It was far better to explain what had happened to the púca than to wait until he found out.

'I'm just going to have a bit of a stroll,' he told Aisling as he went out. He hadn't let her know about the deal with the púca and he had no intention of doing so unless it was entirely necessary.

As he had done before, he hailed the púca from the top meadow of the farm, and, as he had done before, the púca came down to meet JJ in the hazel woods.

'She didn't want to come,' JJ told him anxiously. 'If it was any of the other children I could have just ordered them up here, but Jenny is immune to orders.'

To JJ's astonishment the púca didn't seem bothered at all.

'Don't worry about it, JJ,' he said. 'There's no rush.'

'Really?'

'Really,' said the púca. 'Give her time. Ask her again in a few days and see how she feels.'

'All right,' said JJ, letting out a huge sigh of relief. 'But what if she still doesn't want to?'

'Then leave it again. Wait until she's ready.'

'OK,' said JJ. 'How long have I got?'

'Let's just play it by ear for the moment, shall we?' said the púca. 'We can meet again in a week or so and see how it's going then.'

Mikey was delighted with the stick.

'It's perfect,' he said. 'Absolutely spot on.'

Donal was thrilled, even though he couldn't help noticing that Mikey was holding it upside down, with the helpful bulge near the bottom.

'I feel ten years younger already,' he said, walking across the yard and then back again. 'There's something magical about hazel, isn't there? What was it, now? Did the Salmon of Wisdom eat the hazelnut? Or was it Finn ate the salmon?'

'Didn't he just touch it while it was cooking and then suck his thumb?' said Donal.

'You're right,' said Mikey. 'So where does the hazelnut come in?'

Jenny, who had lingered on in the fort, came round the side of the house.

'Look at this, girleen,' said Mikey, practically striding across the yard, supported by the stick. 'I'll be running with it tomorrow.'

Jenny watched him thoughtfully, but Donal sensed that her thoughts were elsewhere.

'If only this stupid dog would get out of my way,' Mikey was saying, and Donal set off to his rescue.

Relieved of his worries, JJ decided to take a proper walk. He felt slightly guilty about leaving Aidan with Aisling, but if he went back for him now he might get collared to go shopping or help with the housework. All he wanted was a look at the beacon. It wouldn't take long. But when he got there the mountain top beckoned, and this time he did take the long way home, and this time he did visit Coleman's church.

And this time he was entirely successful in forgetting that he was supposed to be making a trip to the railway station.

* * *

As they walked home Donal said to Jenny: 'Do you think we should tell Dad? About this mad idea Mikey has?'

'What mad idea?' said Jenny.

'Climbing to the top of the mountain. Someone ought to stop him.'

'Why?' said Jenny.

'Because he's too old. He'll have a heart attack or something.'

Jenny shrugged. 'I think he'll make it. So does the ghost.'

'The ghost?' said Donal. 'What does the ghost know about Mikey? He can't possibly see Mikey from up there.'

'Not that ghost,' said Jenny. 'The other one.'

'Which other one?' said Donal.

'The one Mikey was talking to when we arrived,' said Jenny. 'The one that lives in his fort.'

11

Luckily Aisling didn't forget the trip to the station. She also went shopping, and she made a roast lamb feast to welcome Hazel home. They waited until Aidan was in bed and asleep before they started, so that they could, for a change, have a peaceful meal.

Hazel was delighted to be home. She had got over the disappointment with Desmond and was keen to start getting out and about again. She said she had been bored witless in Dublin, and she'd had more than enough time to think through the consequences of being a teenage mum. She was glad the whole plan had fallen through.

'But we would have looked after the baby,' said Aisling. 'You knew that.'

'Yeah,' said Hazel, 'but what would my friends have thought? How could I ever have got a decent boyfriend with that kind of baggage tacked on to me?'

'What baby?' said Donal. 'What are you all on about?'

'The baby I was supposed to be having in Dublin,' said Hazel. 'The reason I went away and hid. Their baby.'

Donal was nonplussed and JJ realized that it was time for everybody to be filled in on the whole story. He started at the beginning.

'About twelve years ago I met Aengus Óg and Drowsy Maggie when I was walking in the woods. They had a new baby with them, and Aengus told me that they had come looking for another baby to change it with. The fairy folk have to do that, because there's no way their babies can grow up in Tír na n'Óg.'

'Why not?' said Donal.

'Because there's no time there,' said JJ. 'You can't grow older in a place where there's no time. So they have to swap their baby with someone else's.'

'A changeling,' said Aisling.

'You've heard the old stories,' said JJ. 'The fairies exchange the babies when no one's looking. Well, it really happens, or at least it used to. Then their child grows up with its new parents, and when it's old enough it goes back to Tír na n'Óg.'

'But don't people know that their baby has been swapped?' said Donal. 'Can't they tell?'

'Yes, they can,' said JJ. 'But in the old days there was no way of proving anything, so people just had to put up with it. The problem that Aengus and Maggie were up against is that it's not so easy to do it nowadays. People are much more vigilant than they used to be. More security conscious. They lock their doors at night and they have baby alarms and all that stuff.'

'And photographs,' said Hazel.

'And DNA testing,' said Donal.

'I hadn't thought of that,' said JJ, 'but I suppose that's right. Someone could prove that it wasn't their baby now.'

'And you wouldn't know what they'd find in fairy DNA,' said Hazel.

Everybody laughed, except for Jenny.

'Anyway,' JJ went on, 'your mother and I were expecting a baby ourselves, as it happened. Our second one.'

'Me?' said Donal.

JJ shook his head. 'I had just finished my course in Newark and I was itching to get my hands on some of that chiming maple, so I suggested the deal to Aengus.'

'You'd look after Jenny,' said Donal.

'Exactly.' He laughed again. 'You can imagine what your mother thought about that. I hadn't told her about my visit to Tír na n'Óg and she got hit with it all in one go.'

'I thought he'd gone stark staring mad,' said Aisling. 'I still don't know how he managed to talk me into it.'

'But I did,' said JJ. 'So Aengus and Maggie took their baby back to Tír na n'Óg with them.'

Aisling took up the story. 'And when my baby was born, when it was a few days old, they brought Jenny back and we swapped.'

'But what happened to your baby?' said Donal.

'She went back to Tír na n'Óg with them,' said Aisling. 'She's still a newborn baby now, just a few days old.'

'Wow,' said Donal.

'So that's why we needed Hazel to fake a pregnancy for us. Because if Jenny had gone back to Tír na n'Óg last week and stayed there, JJ would have brought our own baby back.'

'And we would have had to explain her sudden appearance,' said JJ.

But Donal shook his head. 'But she would be the same age as Jenny,' he said.

'She wouldn't,' said JJ, 'because there's no time in Tír na n'Óg. You'd have seen her if we'd gone in there. A beautiful little baby girl.'

'Just as well she was a girl,' said Aisling. 'We would have had trouble explaining that one to the authorities.'

She laughed, and so did JJ and Hazel, but Jenny and Donal were both quite serious.

'But that's there,' said Donal. 'She wouldn't still be a new baby when she came back here. She'd be the same age as Jenny.'

JJ put on his patient-father expression and opened his mouth to explain it all again, but then he stopped. He stared at Donal and his face went pale, and when he glanced across at Aisling his eyes were full of alarm.

'What is it?' she said.

'It's just . . .' he began, but he didn't finish. He looked back at Donal, his mind working frantically.

'JJ?' said Aisling, worried now. 'What is it?'

'But it was you who told me how it works,' said Donal. 'You don't get any older while you're in Tír na n'Óg but your life keeps passing on this side. That's why Father Doherty and Bran died when they came back. Their lives on this side had passed.'

'Is he right, JJ?' Aisling said.

JJ blew air. 'I need to think about this for a minute,' he said.

'Is he, Dad?' said Hazel.

'I am right,' said Donal. 'You know I am.'

'Have you got it wrong?' said Aisling.

'It was Aengus,' said JJ helplessly. 'He put me on the wrong track. He said that when Jenny went home we could have our baby back!'

'And you never worked out that she wouldn't still be a baby?' said Aisling. 'So we're going to be landed with an eleven-year-old?'

'If we are,' said Hazel, 'it will be an eleven-year-old with the mind of a baby. She won't have learned anything, remember?'

'Not an eleven-year-old,' said JJ. 'Jenny isn't going back yet, are you, Jen? Not until you're at least sixteen.'

'That's even worse!' Aisling exploded. 'A sixteen-year-old who can't feed herself or talk! Arriving out of nowhere! How are we going to explain that? And—' Her face crumpled and tears began to gather in the corners of her eyes. 'And I won't have had the chance to see my own baby grow up.'

Everyone was so caught up in the emotional roller-coaster that no one noticed when Jenny quietly pushed back her chair and slipped out of the room. She didn't know exactly where she was going, but she knew that everyone was unhappy, and she believed that it was all her fault. Aisling and JJ had lost their new baby, and all because of her. The boy ghost was up on the mountain, condemned to eternal loneliness. She had befriended him and then abandoned him. The world of the ploddies was a miserable one, full of desires and betrayals. She was ready to leave it all behind and go home to her real father and mother, however feckless and forgetful they might be.

But as she closed the front door behind her she found that an idea had lodged itself in her mind, and by the time she reached the yard gate it was beginning to turn itself into a plan. Perhaps there was a way to make everyone happy.

She thought it through carefully as she walked across Molly's Place, and the plan gradually turned into a resolve. It wasn't going to be easy. It frightened her, and made her legs feel hot and weak. But she was fairly sure she could make it work. However dangerous it might be, Jenny was going to make her own deal with the púca.

12

She didn't even try to look for him. She knew that he would find her, and he did, about halfway between the top meadow of the farm and the stony steps. He lengthened himself and walked beside her to a rocky outcrop where they would both find comfortable seats.

'I'm so pleased you came,' he said. 'I was afraid you wouldn't ever come back and see me.'

Jenny was breathing hard, more from fear than from the exertion of the climb. She waited until the púca had settled himself on a slab of limestone, then she leaned against a boulder a few paces away from him.

'I heard you wanted to see me,' she said. 'What was it about?'

'Why should it have been about anything?' he said. 'I used to enjoy our lessons and our little chats. I missed you, that was all.'

'I didn't think anybody cared about me,' said Jenny.

'Not since I found out why I'm here. You knew all along, didn't you?'

The púca tried to make a sympathetic face, but it looked pretty stupid on a goat. It was almost dark by now but the púca's shaggy coat was so white and clean that she had no trouble seeing him.

'People have let you down badly, haven't they, Jenny?' he said.

Jenny nodded.

'It's no surprise to me,' he went on. 'You don't belong with them and you never did. They let everyone down, that lot, even each other.'

Jenny nodded again. 'They're a bit of a disaster,' she said.

'That's putting it mildly,' said the púca. 'There never was a race of creatures like them.' His eyes took on a dreamy expression. 'Oh, this used to be such a beautiful place, Jenny. I wish you had seen it in the old days. Healthy forests and fresh air. No cities, no cars, no aeroplanes, no filth.'

'It must have been lovely,' said Jenny.

'It was,' said the púca. 'Of all the worlds, this one was the most glorious. Our finest creation, and our favourite. But look at it now. Look at the mess they've made of it.'

Jenny looked at it, or at least she looked at the tiny bit of it that she could see in the darkness.

'But you aren't one of them,' he went on. 'You know that now, so we can talk more freely. You are more like me than like them. You come from a race of gods.'

'Do I?' said Jenny. 'Does that mean I'm a god?'

'A godling, perhaps. Do you have any powers?'

'I don't know,' said Jenny. 'I can't make people dizzy, anyway.'

'Never mind,' said the púca. 'It might come to you later. But there is another kind of power that I know you have.'

'Really?' said Jenny. 'What's that?'

The púca gave a great sigh and said, 'You were right, Jenny. There is a reason that I wanted to talk to you. The ruination of this world has to stop, and you may be the only one who can stop it.'

'Me?' said Jenny. 'How?'

'I want you to use your influence with the ghost,' said the púca. 'I want you to persuade him to leave.'

13

Hazel stood in the middle of the kitchen assessing the ruins of the family reunion. Her mother had gone up to bed in floods of tears. Her father was sitting at the table with his head in his hands and hadn't moved for twenty minutes. Donal, clearly quite pleased with himself for having caused it all, was playing with his gamepod in the armchair beside the range.

'Where's Jenny?' As she said it, Hazel's mind raced back over the whole conversation and she saw how it must have appeared from Jenny's point of view. Everyone's focus had been on the baby and its eventual return to the family. No one had given a moment's consideration to Jenny's feelings.

She checked in the sitting room and the bedrooms, then went out into the yard and called. In the still evening air her voice carried easily across the half-mile or so that lay between the house and the place where Jenny and the púca were talking. Both of them ignored it.

'What will happen to the ploddies if I get rid of the ghost and you get the hatchet back?' Jenny was saying.

The púca could barely conceal a gleeful grin. 'Their number will be up at last,' he said. 'They'll hardly know what hit them.'

'What, all of them?'

'Well, not all of them exactly. We would want to keep a few of them around to graft the apple trees and cultivate root vegetables.' He paused for a moment and licked his chops with a long pink tongue. 'But there would have to be a serious reduction in their numbers before this world got back into balance again.' He waited, and when Jenny said nothing he went on, 'Is there someone in particular you'd like us to spare?'

'I think so,' said Jenny. 'I know the Liddys aren't perfect but they're the only family I ever knew.'

'Right,' said the púca. 'We'll leave the Liddys alone.'

'Including all the grandparents, and Marian in Cork, and her husband Danny.'

'That can be arranged,' said the púca.

'And all the people in my school,' said Jenny.

'OK.'

'Actually,' said Jenny, 'would you mind sparing everyone in Kinvara? It's not a very big place.'

'I think we could manage that,' said the púca. 'They would probably spread out a bit after a while. Is that all?'

'And Maureen the archaeologist who brought me a

cup of coffee on the beacon,' said Jenny. 'But I don't know where she lives.'

'We'll find her,' said the púca, 'and we'll spare her. I have a mental note of all that.'

'What will you do to the other people, then?' said Jenny. 'Everybody else?'

'Well,' said the púca, 'the terms of the peace agreement made no mention of undercover warfare, so we have been using those all along. Floods, hurricanes, famines, diseases, that kind of thing. But once the hatchet is out from under that slagheap we can go back to direct action.' He smiled at Jenny. 'We'll be able to return to our original shapes.'

Jenny remembered the images of the big lizardy things the ghost had shown her. The scales, the horns, the claws.

'Which are . . . ?' she said.

The púca smiled again, and this time a glint of fiery red light showed in his throat. She saw fangs in the goat mouth. She knew.

'Did you never wonder why it is that human beings have no predator?' he said. 'They did have, once, but only their old stories remember us now. When we are free to do battle again they will remember our power. One of us on the rampage can make short work of a little town like Ennis. Three of us could flatten Dublin inside a day.'

'But not the Dublin grandparents,' said Jenny, battling to keep her nerve. 'You won't flatten them.'

'Not the Dublin grandparents,' said the púca patiently. 'They're on my list.'

For a long time Jenny said nothing. The púca waited until, finally, his patience ran out. 'So what do you think?' he said.

'I think I would be very scared of your original shape,' said Jenny.

'But it won't be turned against you.'

'No, I suppose not.'

'So what do you think?' said the púca. 'Will you do it? Will you go and have a chat with the ghost?'

14

JJ stumbled uselessly around the hillside for half an hour but drew the line at entering the woods. He called out a couple of times from the edge, but it was dark enough out in the open, and who knew what might be waiting for him in there? In any case, it was possible that he had just missed Jenny. There was every chance that she had made her own way home by now.

She hadn't, though. Aisling had got up again and had lit the range in anticipation of a long night. Hazel, having done all she could to try and find Jenny, was in the armchair busily texting friends. Donal was finishing off the apple crumble.

'We could phone the police,' said Aisling, 'if I hadn't so cleverly cried wolf all summer.'

'I don't see what the police could do anyway,' said JJ. 'No one's going to find her in the dark.'

'We ought to have a dog,' said Hazel. 'If we had a dog it would find her.'

Donal put the empty pie-dish in the sink and sucked the spoon. 'I don't know what all the fuss is about,' he said. 'Jenny is a fairy, isn't she? She's perfectly capable of looking after herself.'

Which was, JJ had to admit, the most sensible thing anybody had said all evening. No one knew the mountainside as well as Jenny did, and if she met the púca up there, well, wasn't that exactly what JJ wanted?

'I tell you what,' said Jenny. 'I'll make a deal with you.'

The púca looked startled, but he quickly regained his composure and said, 'Go on. I'm listening.'

'Well,' said Jenny, 'the thing is, there's been this stupid mix-up over a baby in Tír na n'Óg. My other half. The one I was swapped for.'

'What kind of mix-up?'

'Her mother expected her to still be a baby when we changed back, but they got it wrong. She won't be. She'll be the same age as me, won't she? The same age she would be if she had stayed here?'

'She will,' said the púca. 'That's the way I understand it, anyway.'

'So, I know you made some wood get older for JJ. Could you fix it so that the baby doesn't get older when she comes out of Tír na n'Óg?'

'Ooh,' said the púca. 'Tall order.' He scratched an ear with his long elegant fingers and creased his hairy brow. He uncrossed his legs and crossed them again with the under one over. He turned his lizard eyes up to the dark sky and back down to his white lap. While he thought, night creatures rustled along the forest floor and in the trees above them.

'Make someone younger,' he mused.

'Not make her younger,' said Jenny. 'Just stop her getting older.'

'Hmm,' said the púca, and after a moment or two he said, 'Hmm,' again. Then he said, 'Do you know, I think it can be done. In fact she probably wouldn't have survived coming back in the normal way. Increasing your size and bodyweight instantly by something of the order of two thousand per cent is almost certain to be fatal. But if we do it my way we can keep her small and keep her alive. It will involve taking her through a series of worlds, including one where she will be temporarily turned into a gas and one in which time goes backwards, but it will work, I'm certain of that.'

'Excellent!' said Jenny. 'And can you do a straight swap? Bring her back from Tír na n'Óg as soon as the ghost is gone?'

The púca considered this. 'I can probably contrive a causative link between the two events, yes.'

'And can you have her just appear? In my bedroom, say?'

'No, Jenny,' said the púca, without hesitation. 'That would be magic, and magic is beyond me. I am less restricted than most creatures but I'm still bound by the laws of nature, and so is the baby. But I could probably arrange to have her delivered to your doorstep.'

'That'll do,' said Jenny. 'Is it a deal, then? I persuade the boy ghost to leave the beacon and you get the baby home?'

'It's a deal,' said the púca.

'And you'll spare the Liddys and all the grandparents, and Marian and Danny?'

'I'll spare every last one of them.'

'And everyone in Kinvara?'

'And everyone in Kinvara.'

'And Maureen the archaeologist who brought me a cup of coffee on the beacon?'

'And Maureen the archaeologist who brought you a cup of coffee on the beacon. On my honour.'

The púca's honour was enough for Jenny, and she stretched out her hand. The púca took it in his, and the agreement was sealed.

15

Jenny left the púca in the woods and walked up the hillside. The sky was cloudy and the half-moon appeared only occasionally, but there was still enough light for her to see where she was going. She had her own particular way of getting up to the beacon, following paths made by the wild goats and skirting around the stony steps to avoid the steepest climbs. The night was cool and damp and not at all frightening. It held a rich assortment of smells of the sort you never got in daylight. She saw a fox and two badgers, all very close, none of them in the least bit afraid of her. Darkness was their territory.

The ghost, too, seemed stronger in the night. Although she still couldn't see him with the front part of her eyes, his form in her peripheral vision was well-defined and consistent. He was surprised to see her there, but very pleased. It was many days since she had paid him a visit, and ghost days are no shorter than ploddy ones.

Jenny sat on her favourite stone and watched clouds drifting across the one-eyed moon. For a long time she thought about the púca and its fighting form, and she wondered whether she really had the courage to go through with the deal. She had wronged the boy ghost by believing him to be deluded and she wanted to put it right by delivering him from his misery and loneliness. And the strange thing was that all along, without her ever knowing it, the púca had been providing her with the means of doing it.

She followed her thoughts in one direction and another. They always arrived back at the same place. She had made an agreement with the púca and, whatever else he might be, the púca was honourable. Of that she was certain. And since she was a godling, she must be honourable, too. She would keep her end of the bargain to the letter and the word.

She took a swig of dark mountain air, and began to talk to the ghost.

For half the summer's night they talked about the world as the boy had known it and the world as it was now. They talked about people past and people present, about how they lived then and how they lived now, about what their needs had been then and what they had become. They talked about where need ended and where greed began. Jenny told the ghost what she had learned from reading the winds, though she didn't tell him how she had learned it. She told him about the things he couldn't see: the massive cities drinking energy night and day, the planes taking off and returning like bees around a hive, the people who had forgotten how to walk because they drove everywhere in cars. She told him about the melting ice-caps and the hole in the ozone layer and the species that were becoming extinct before they had even been discovered and given a name. And as she talked he questioned her, and she sensed the first fault-lines beginning to appear in the ghost's conviction. In all his twelve years as a boy and his thousands of years as a ghost he had never doubted the absolute right of human beings to use the earth in whatever way they pleased. But then, in all those thousands of years, he had never heard anything like the things that Jenny was telling him now.

She chose her words and her topics carefully. She knew that if she pushed too hard and too fast it might have the opposite effect to what she intended. It was very important that she didn't alienate the ghost and lose his trust. So she sweetened the bitter pill from time to time by talking about the good things in human nature; about friendship and generosity and the spirit of co-operation. They talked about people who chose to go against the trend and live simple lives, and people who devoted their time to helping others. And they talked about poetry and music, which the gods loved as much as people did, and which ghosts loved, too.

By the time Jenny got up to leave she was fairly sure that she had got the tone just right. The ghost wasn't going anywhere just yet, but the total conviction that had kept him attached to the earth for all those thousands of years had been seriously undermined. He had glimpsed the possibility of escape, and although he wasn't about to take it just yet, Jenny was as sure as she could be that he would be ready to go when, or if, the rest of her plan fell into place.

So she was full of high spirits when she got back to the house in the early hours of the morning, and not at all prepared for the reception that was awaiting her. Gushing with relief, JJ and Aisling took turns in hugging her tight, and kissing her, and telling her how worried they had been.

'I'm a godling,' she said to them sternly. 'I'm well able to look after myself.'

But she couldn't help feeling just a little bit fond of them. She was glad that she'd made the púca promise to spare them. If her plan worked properly, it wouldn't be necessary, but there was no harm in having a safe-guard built in, just in case.

'Um, Jenny?' said JJ as they were all heading up to bed.

'Yes?'

'I was just wondering. Did you happen to meet the púca tonight?'

'Yep,' said Jenny.

JJ grinned with delight, but Jenny wondered whether his grin would be so wide if he had heard what she and the púca had agreed.

The púca, all too well aware of her credentials, had not entirely trusted Jenny when they made their deal. The fairy folk were notorious for their trickery, and even a juvenile might prove untrustworthy. But when he visited the mountain top at dawn he was very well pleased with what he found. The ghost was still there but his power had waned. His area of influence had receded dramatically, and the púca was able to get a lot closer to the beacon than before. With enormous satisfaction he grazed in grassy hollows where he hadn't set foot for more than three thousand years.

16

Jenny slept until eight o'clock the next morning, which was unprecedented. Aisling and JJ were not so lucky. Aidan woke at his usual time of seven o'clock and they both got up with him, hoping to catch Jenny before she went out.

By the time they had finished their breakfast everyone was up except for Hazel, who rarely emerged before lunch time. JJ persuaded Donal to take Aidan for a walk so that he and Aisling could have some time with Jenny on her own.

'We wanted to have a bit of a chat about things,' said JJ.

'What things?' said Jenny.

'Well, about everything. About you being . . . er . . . adopted and everything. Now that you know.'

Jenny was quite relieved that the chat wasn't going to be about the púca and the ghosts. That was something she wanted to keep to herself.

'We ought to have talked things over with you long before this,' said Aisling, 'instead of just springing it on you last week.'

'I shouldn't have tried to take you back to Tír na n'Óg,' said JJ. 'That was a mistake.'

Jenny shrugged and looked out of the window. 'I don't mind going there,' she said.

'But we don't want you to, Jen,' said Aisling. 'We want you to stay here with us.'

'Why?'

'Because we'd miss you if you weren't here. We don't want you to go to Tír na n'Óg until you're good and ready.'

'I'm good and ready now,' said Jenny. 'Nearly.' She was intrigued by Tír na n'Óg now that she had learned a bit more about it. She wished she had taken the opportunity to get to know Aengus Óg that day instead of running away from him.

'Thing is,' said JJ, 'you're not really ready to go back there yet.'

'Then why did you try to take me?'

'I was annoyed with Aengus because he hadn't given me the wood for my fiddles. I wasn't thinking straight.'

'Neither of us were,' said Aisling. 'We want you to understand that you're part of our family and you'll stay part of it, just like the others, until you're grown up and ready to leave home.'

'I'm ready to leave home now,' said Jenny. 'Nearly.'

'Well, we don't agree,' said JJ. 'We don't think you're big enough.'

'Why do I have to be big?'

'Because none of the changelings go back to Tír na n'Óg until they're grown up. Everyone there is an adult.'

'Oh,' said Jenny, looking out of the window again. The hillside was bright with late summer sunshine, and it was beckoning. 'Can I go out now?'

'Yes, you can, Jen,' said Aisling. 'But listen. Will you forgive us for behaving so stupidly?'

'Yes, I will,' said Jenny. 'I already have.'

'And will you do one more thing?' said JJ.

'What?' said Jenny.

'Will you promise not to go out at night again?'

Jenny thought about this and remembered her godling status and her newly acquired sense of honour. She couldn't lie. So she said, quite calmly, 'No. I like going out at night.'

Donal took Aidan all the way to Mikey's house but they didn't stay long. Aidan tried to pull Belle's ears off, and when that didn't work he started slamming the poker into the slumbering fire, sending up powdery explosions of sparks and pinky-grey ash.

'I won't bring him again,' said Donal, hauling his protesting brother towards the front door.

'Don't mind him,' said Mikey. 'He's only young. He'll learn. But come again, you, tomorrow morning. I want you for something.'

'OK,' said Donal. 'Will I bring the accordion?'

'Best leave it at home this time,' said Mikey. 'But come good and early, will you?'

JJ met them at the bottom of the drive, where he was clearing years of sediment out of the cattle grid. It was effectively useless, but they would need it to be working when the cattle arrived the next day.

'How is Mikey?' he asked Donal.

'He's good,' said Donal. 'He was asking for you.'

'I must call down to him one of the days,' said JJ. 'I must bring the fiddle down and play him a few tunes.'

'You should definitely go,' said Donal. 'But I don't think he's so interested in tunes any more.'

'No?' said JJ.

'No,' said Donal. 'He seems to have something else on his mind.'

17

Jenny sat on the hillside above the farm and watched
the traffic moving along the New Line. There wasn't very
much of it. A couple of cars, then a gap, then a tractor
and trailer, then another long gap, then another couple
of cars. Sometimes as much as five minutes would go by
with nothing moving in either direction. She tried to
guess what would come next, but she never got it right.

A hare ambled past, seeming not to notice her. Soon
afterwards the white goat appeared and came over to
sit beside her.

'Well done, little Jenny,' he said.

It was too exposed for the púca to change shape, and
he never spoke so clearly when he was entirely goat.
Jenny supposed it must be difficult to make the
sounds come out right with such a long jaw.

'Well done for what?' she said.

'For talking to the ghost,' said the púca. 'You're
definitely getting somewhere.'

'It wasn't so hard,' said Jenny.

'How much longer will it take, do you think?'

Jenny shrugged. 'Slowly slowly catchee monkey.'

'And what is that supposed to mean?'

'Can't rush these things,' said Jenny. 'That ghost has been there for a long, long time.' She pulled up a stalk of grass and chewed the sweet pulp at its base. 'Have you sorted something out about the baby?'

'I have,' said the púca. 'I have organized an envoy to bring her back the instant the ghost lets go.'

'Wonderful,' said Jenny. 'So everything's on track.'

'Will it be days?' said the púca. 'Weeks? Months?'

'One of those or all of them,' said Jenny nonchalantly. 'There's no point in nagging me.'

The púca accepted this without a word. He got up and shook himself, then wandered back towards the woods.

Jenny let out a long breath. She wasn't anywhere near as calm as she had let on. Her plan depended on one essential thing over which she had no control. All she could do now was wait and hope that it would happen.

18

Donal woke to the sound of his mother trying to get Hazel out of bed. He lay listening for a moment or two, then jumped up and got dressed.

He knew why Hazel had to get up. Aisling and JJ were both going to the mart in Ennistymon to look at cattle and possibly to buy some. Hazel had promised to mind Aidan for the day, but she had been out clubbing the night before and she had undoubtedly got back very late. It meant that Donal had to make himself scarce as soon as he could, because there was a very strong chance that he would be dragged in to deputize until Hazel got up.

In the kitchen JJ was buttering toast and Aidan, who was always at his most co-operative in the mornings, was carrying a carton of milk from the fridge to the table. Before JJ had even registered that he was there, Donal had collected two slices of toast and his hazel stick, and had slipped out through the back door. He ate the toast as he walked down the drive in the weak morning sunshine. It was only seven o'clock.

Well, Mikey had told him to come early.

Jenny was already up on her perch on the hillside. She had been up there when the rubbish lorry passed on its way from Carron to Kinvara, and when the first commuter traffic had come up in the other direction and turned down the New Line towards Ennis.

So far the púca hadn't made an appearance, and Jenny strongly suspected that he wouldn't, since she had scolded him for nagging. He was well capable of being patient. He had waited for three thousand years, after all, so what difference would a few more days make, here or there? As for herself, though, a few days seemed like a lifetime.

She stifled a yawn and watched a big white van speeding along the New Line from the Ballyvaughan direction. The next one, she decided, would be a blue four-by-four heading towards Kinvara. It was a red hatchback, heading towards Carron.

After another half an hour and another forty-two cars and vans, Jenny walked up to the beacon to see how the ghost was getting on. He was pleased to see her, but was clearly depressed. She was very careful not to talk about anything gloomy, and by the time she left he seemed a bit more cheerful, and Jenny was glad of that.

As she walked back down the mountainside she mused on her new-found ability to understand what other people were feeling. In some ways she liked it – it added a whole new dimension to life and to her relationships with others. But in another way it was a dreadful inconvenience. It was sympathy for the ghost and sympathy for Aisling that had led her to devise this plan. And while it was very exciting, it was dangerous as well, and there were moments when she wondered whether she hadn't bitten off more than she could chew, godling or no godling. If it went pear-shaped she could be in all kinds of trouble when she got back home.

They were halfway to Ennistymon when Aisling said: 'We really should have brought someone with us who knows something about cattle. We'll probably end up buying something with false teeth or asthma.'

'Nonsense,' said JJ. 'I was born and bred a farmer. Don't forget that.'

'But you kept goats, JJ. Not cattle. There are differences, you know.'

'Not significant ones. A healthy beast is a healthy beast, no matter what size it is.'

'All the same,' said Aisling, 'I was just thinking how nice it would have been if we could have brought Mikey. He would have enjoyed it, too.'

'God, he would,' said JJ. 'And no better man to cast an eye over cattle.'

They fell silent for a while, each of them thinking about Mikey. 'I wonder, is it too late to go back and get him?' said JJ.

'It is a bit,' said Aisling. 'We couldn't just expect him to drop everything and come with us. But we don't have to buy anything today. We can just look. Bring Mikey with us next time.'

'Bit of a waste of time borrowing the trailer, then, wasn't it?' said JJ.

In any event they would have been wasting their time if they had gone back for Mikey. He wasn't there. As Jenny came down from the beacon she spotted him heading towards her with Donal at his side. They had already crossed the New Line and were making their way over the pastureland that lay outside the boundaries of the Liddy farm, on the Ballyvaughan side. They hadn't yet reached the steep part of the incline but even so the old man was making heavy weather of it, taking a few small steps at a time and leaning hard on his stick.

Jenny looked around, made a quick assessment of the situation, then went down to help them.

* * *

Donal tried to think of things to say to Mikey as they made their slow way up the hillside. He had already gone through every variation of 'this is not a good idea' that he could dream up, but Mikey had not responded to any of them. He had no shortage of time in which to reply but he did have a severe shortage of breath and he wasn't prepared to waste any of it on arguments.

Instead he ploughed on doggedly, concentrating on putting one foot in front of the other, and doing his best not to look up too often in case the prospect of the climb ahead robbed him of his resolve.

'Mum and Dad have gone to Ennistymon,' said Donal.

Mikey nodded, but said nothing.

'To buy cattle,' Donal went on.

Mikey stopped. He leaned on his stick and breathed hard for a few minutes. Donal saw the high colour in his face and wondered again how to stop this mad enterprise.

'That's the best news I heard in fifteen years,' said Mikey at last. 'A farmer without stock is like a donkey with no legs. Going nowhere fast. I never thought I'd see the day when the Liddys stopped farming and I'm glad I lived to see them come to their senses. It'll fall to you, of course, when JJ's over the hill.'

'It might not,' said Donal. 'Hazel might take over.'

'That girl isn't a farmer and nor is Jenny. But you

are, Donal. It was written all over you from the day you were born. I never doubted it for a minute.'

'I thought I might be a musician,' said Donal. 'Like Dad.'

'And so you will be,' said Mikey. 'But you can be a farmer as well.'

He looked up at the mountainside and Donal caught a momentary expression of despair in his milky blue eyes. Then it was gone. He planted his hazel rod firmly and started forward again.

There was a stone wall that ran across the top of the meadow and separated it from the wilder, stonier mountainside above. Jenny reached that wall before Mikey and Donal did, and it was immediately obvious to her that the old man would never be able to climb over it. So, instead of getting over and going on to meet them, Jenny stayed where she was and, carefully and methodically, knocked down a two-metre length of it. By the time the others reached her there was a clear gap without a single loose stone to impede their progress. Mikey gave Jenny a lopsided grin and heaved himself painfully through it.

'Why did you do that?' Donal hissed at her under his breath. 'If he couldn't get over we might have been able to stop him!'

'Why would you want to stop him?' said Jenny.

'Why are you helping him if you don't want him to go?'

'Because I don't want him to be on his own.'

'Well, he isn't. You can go back now, if you want.'

Donal shook his head and went back to Mikey's side. The ground was getting steeper and rougher, and the old man was going to need all the help he could get.

19

The weather, as it turned out, could not have been better if they had ordered it. There were few clouds and no prospect of rain, but it wasn't too hot, either. Inch by inch, step by painful step, Mikey struggled on up the mountain. He took frequent rests and, as the day wore on, the time he spent walking decreased and the time he spent recovering increased. Patiently the children shuffled along beside him, helping him over rocks and grikes, taking it in turns to hold him by the elbow and steer him on the easiest course.

'The stick's the thing,' he said, during one of his longer breaks. 'I'd never have got this far without it.'

As midday approached, Donal left his stick with Jenny and ran down as far as the house for a flask of tea and some sandwiches. During the hour that he was gone Mikey and Jenny barely covered another hundred metres, so he had no difficulty in finding them again. They didn't bother to try and find a level spot for their picnic but sat down exactly where they were on the stony slope. Mikey stretched out flat on his back, his bony chest heaving beneath his cotton shirt, and Donal was afraid that he was going to die. But after a few minutes he sat up again, and a bit of the old sparkle had returned to his eye.

He grinned at Donal. 'By God,' he said, 'but old age isn't for sissies!'

Around the time they were having their lunch, Nancy McGrath was making her daily visit to Mikey's house. Belle greeted her enthusiastically but there was no sign of Mikey, and Nancy walked anxiously through the house, checking each room in turn. When she didn't find him she tried the yard and the haggard, and then took a quick scout around the neighbouring fields. She generally knew if Mikey was planning to go some-where, and if he went out unexpectedly he usually left a note. She thought about it now and she didn't recall him mentioning anything. But there was no sign that anything was amiss, so she put the dog back into the house and went home.

The sandwiches and tea had a great effect on Mikey and, as soon as they were finished, he announced that he was ready to continue. It took both children all their strength to haul him to his feet again, but once he was upright he appeared to be steady enough. He looked up towards the stony steps and back the way they had come.

'We're doing better than I thought,' he said. 'We're well over halfway there.'

They were, too. The next part of the climb was the steepest of all, but after that it would be all level going across the flat summit to the beacon. The stony steps were going to be a struggle, but even so, it occurred to Donal for the first time that Mikey was actually going to make it. The realization brought about a complete reversal in his attitude. He didn't want to stop Mikey any more. He was determined to help him get up to the beacon.

20

They had barely started out again when the white goat came bounding across the hillside and stopped a few metres ahead of them, blocking their way. Mikey swore under his breath.

'That flaming thing is still here,' he said to the children. 'Seventy years I've been coming up this mountain and not a day passed but I didn't see that goat. It isn't natural. No goat could live that long.'

'What do you want?' said Jenny to the púca.

'Why are you bringing that old man up the mountain?' he replied.

She was surprised that he had answered her and turned to Mikey to gauge his reaction. He was speechless; staring at the púca with his mouth open.

'I'm not bringing him up,' said Jenny. 'He decided to come up and I decided to help him.'

'I see,' said the púca. 'What a coincidence. Here you

are on the mountainside and you just happen to meet up with the last of the High Kings.'

'He isn't a king,' said Jenny. 'Ireland doesn't have a king. Mikey has been up here millions of times. He owns the land up here.'

The púca snorted, a short, sharp pellet of sound that ricocheted around the hillside. 'That old arrogance again!' he barked. 'How can a human being own land? Of all their follies, that one is the greatest. No one owns the land, fairy child. No one except for us.'

'There's no use talking to it!' said Mikey, who had recovered the power of speech and was quivering with fear and rage. 'There's only one way to deal with a goat!'

He took a step forward and made a brave attempt to brandish his stick. Unfortunately he had become dependent upon it for keeping his balance, and if the children hadn't reacted instantly to save him he would have pitched forward and landed on his face.

The púca laughed.

'It isn't funny,' said Jenny. 'Let us pass.'

'You can pass, Jenny. You and the Liddy boy. But he can't.'

'But why not? He's just an old man.'

'An old man with a very long history behind him,' said the púca. 'It was the first of his line who thwarted us in those negotiations all those years ago. It was his ancestor that set the ghost to guard the hatchet.'

'But Mikey doesn't know anything about all that stuff,' said Donal, and Jenny could see a mixture of terror and fury on his face. 'He just wants to see the place one last time.'

'That's right,' said Jenny. 'Where's the harm in that?'

'I don't know,' said the púca, 'and I have no intention of finding out.'

'Let us pass!' said Donal.

The púca said nothing, but dropped his horns in an extremely threatening manner.

'You're not allowed to hurt us,' said Jenny, but she wasn't as sure as she sounded. The peace agreement wouldn't allow the púca to attack them in its real form, it was true, but if he was just a goat, a simple creature, would that count? Or was that another example of undercover warfare?

Donal took a step forward. The goat did the same. There were barely ten metres between them.

'Careful now,' said Mikey. 'Don't enrage him.'

But Donal had succumbed to his anger. He raised his stick and swung it from side to side in front of him. In reply, the púca propped forwards, head down, in a gesture that promised an imminent charge.

'Daddy!' Jenny yelled.

'Whisht, child,' said Mikey. 'How can your daddy hear you all the way from Ennistymon?'

Jenny didn't reply. She cupped her hands around her mouth and yelled again. 'Daddeeeee!!!'

As it happened, JJ was not in Ennistymon. He and Aisling had looked at cattle until they developed brown spots in front of their eyes. They had talked to farmers, dealers and butchers, and had received so much advice, most of it conflicting, that their brains were addled and their nerve was completely shaken. They watched the first few lots go through the auction ring to get an idea of prices, then they went back to the car and set out for home.

But it wasn't JJ that Jenny had been calling. Which was just as well. The goat was advancing upon Donal, who was standing his ground and waving the stick in a way that was very brave but also very foolhardy. He had painted himself into a corner and there was nowhere for him to run. Behind him, Jenny was try-ing to manoeuvre Mikey out of the line of charge but Mikey was glued to the spot, staring in horror at the scene of impending disaster.

Jenny yelled for her father one final time. The goat snorted and stood on his hind legs, preparing to attack. With that extra bit of height, his enormous weight and the advantage of his uphill position, he would have hit Donal with the force of a speeding motorbike. But in a sudden terrifying tornado of black wings a huge raven appeared, its beak and claws aimed with deadly accuracy at the púca's eyes.

The goat bawled. He ducked and twisted and fell heavily on his side, knocking Donal off his feet and rolling on to land in a heap beside Mikey and Jenny. The raven pursued him, still pecking and clawing, and the huge wings drove Jenny backwards, away from the fracas. The goat gained his feet, tossed his horns at the raven, then bounded away across the hillside. The raven hovered for a moment and then, in front of the astonished watchers, turned itself into a man.

21

'I knew you'd come,' said Jenny to Aengus, grinning from ear to ear.

Donal had picked himself up and was helping Mikey to lower himself on to a rock. The old man had a hand clutched to his chest and was sucking hard at his breath.

'What on earth is going on?' said Aengus, a little crossly. 'How did you get yourself into this mess?'

'We're helping Mikey up the mountain,' said Jenny cheerfully.

'But why?' said Aengus.

'Because he wants to go.'

To Donal's relief, Mikey was recovering himself. 'By God,' he said. 'I've seen everything now.'

'Have you?' said Aengus pithily. 'Then perhaps it's time for you to go home.'

Mikey laughed. 'First a talking goat and then you.

One minute a crow and the next minute a man. That takes the biscuit.'

'A raven, as a matter of fact,' said Aengus. 'Significantly different, both factually and symbolically.' He turned away from Mikey and smiled sweetly at Jenny. 'But anyway, are you all right now? Anything else you need?'

'Are you going?' said Jenny. 'What's the hurry?'

'I was dancing a set,' said Aengus. 'They'll be a man short.'

'Well, too bad,' said Jenny. 'They'll just have to find another one.'

Aengus's eyes flashed. 'Oh?' he said. 'And who says so?'

'I do,' said Jenny. 'You promised you'd help me if I was in trouble.'

'And I did!' said Aengus, with an injured air.

'Well, I'm still in trouble,' said Jenny. 'That púca isn't just going to go away, you know. I need you to help us take Mikey to the top of the mountain. All the way to the beacon, in fact.'

Aengus gave an extremely disgruntled sigh, and Jenny went on: 'Daddy! You have all the time in the world for dancing!'

'Actually that's not true,' said Aengus. 'The thing about time is—'

'Give me a hand up there, young fella,' said Mikey, cutting in.

Aengus gave Jenny a withering stare but Jenny refused to wither. So he reached out a hand and, with the greatest of ease, pulled Mikey to his feet.

Mikey rubbed his hands together and accepted his stick from Donal.

'This is great,' he said. 'We'll fly up there now with the bit of extra help.'

'Oh,' said Aengus, his voice oily with mock respect. 'And would sir prefer to fly?'

'No, no,' said Mikey hastily. 'Walking will do fine.'

'Good,' said Aengus, and he turned Mikey into a pig.

22

Nancy McGrath went back to Mikey's house to see if he had returned. She checked all the rooms again, and then the yard and the haggard, and this time she went through all the ramshackle old outbuildings as well. When she still found no trace of Mikey she phoned JJ's mobile.

'No, he's not here,' said JJ. 'He's probably not far away.'

He listened while Nancy explained that she had checked on him twice, and that he never went anywhere without letting her know. He still wasn't worried, but Hazel was in a huff about something and Aidan was on the rampage, and he didn't need too much persuasion to get out of the house.

'You go on home,' he said, 'and I'll pop down there in an hour or so. It's high time I paid Mikey a visit, anyway.'

*   *   *

Jenny wasn't sure about the logic of turning Mikey into a pig. It certainly hadn't had any effect upon the speed of their ascent. The pig was every bit as wheezy and arthritic as Mikey had been and just as reluctant to go more than a few steps at a time.

Donal was at the front, guiding the pig by holding one of its ears. 'I don't think this is fair,' he said to Aengus. 'Why did you turn him into a pig?'

Aengus was at the back, leaning on the pig's meaty rump, heaving it forwards. 'I don't like pushing old men around the place,' he said. 'Pigs, for some reason, are not so easily offended.'

The pig tottered on a few steps then stopped again, panting.

'But why a pig?' said Jenny. 'Why not something smaller and easier to manage? If you turned him into a hare we could carry him up.'

'It's a bodyweight thing, erm . . . er . . .'

'Jenny,' said Jenny.

'Jenny,' said Aengus. 'The very young and the very old don't fare well with sudden alterations. All right for the likes of you and me' – he winked at her – 'but ploddies are frail and easily shocked.'

He aimed a kick at the pig's backside but an angry glare from Donal persuaded him to think better of it. 'Besides,' he went on, 'the last time I turned a ploddy into a hare it ran off into the heather and was never seen again.'

Jenny laughed, thinking about a teacher she particularly disliked. 'Would I be able to do that?' she said. 'Change people into other things?'

'You would indeed,' said Aengus, 'if you had a bit of practice. And púcas, too, although they're much harder. They require a more specialized kind of art.'

'You can do it to púcas? Is that why they're afraid of you?'

Aengus hissed and shuddered. 'They hate us with a vengeance, Jenny. It takes a lot of skill and energy to change a púca and it's only ever to be used as a last resort. If you got it wrong you could knock the whole planet off its hinges and set it drifting in outer space.'

'Wow,' said Jenny.

'Yes, wow,' said Aengus. 'So don't you even think about trying it.'

'I won't,' said Jenny.

'Good,' said Aengus. 'Now give me a hand with this pig!'

Up on the beacon the lonely ghost was in difficulty. Everything looked just as it had always looked, but he could sense the gathering of powerful forces beyond the horizon.

He thought about Jenny and wondered whether he

had been right to trust her. The trouble was, if she had tricked him she had done it much too well. He had lost the absolute faith in humanity that had kept him there for all those years, and all his efforts to regain it had led to nothing. The truth was that he was tired. He had been ready to hear an excuse for him to leave this desolate post. And now that his determination had weakened and his power had waned, he wasn't at all sure whether he could withstand the onslaught that he feared was about to be unleashed.

JJ opened the case and looked at his fiddle for the first time since he had returned from the USA. He was appalled by the state it was in. The belly was covered with sticky white rosin and the strings were worn out and dead. As well as that, the pegs were sticking right through the peg box and badly needed replacing. It was a dreadful way to treat an instrument that was one of the finest ever made, and it was a very poor advertisement for someone who had set himself up as a maker and restorer. Ashamed of himself, he zipped up the case, shouldered it and set out for Mikey's house.

As he walked down the drive his spirits lifted and he began to forgive himself. He had been under pressure with all the touring and recording but from now on his life was going to be different. He was looking forward to the cattle and to getting the workshop in order. He was looking forward to the classes and céilís starting up again in a few weeks' time. And most of all he was looking forward to spending more time with Aisling and the children. He was glad that Jenny wasn't going back to Tír na n'Óg. He had never taken the trouble to get to know her properly, and of all the priorities that were piled up in the front of his mind, Jenny was the highest.

As Nancy McGrath had done, JJ let himself into the house and checked through all the rooms. He looked around the yard and the haggard and the outbuildings and then, reluctant to go straight home, he took a stroll around the fields of Mikey's home farm. There were cattle there, belonging to Peter Hayes, and JJ cast an appraising eye over them. He wondered again whether he could ask Mikey for a lease on the winterage above his own farm. He knew Peter Hayes hadn't renewed it that year, but he didn't know why.

JJ stopped and looked up there, and that was when he saw the three figures, and what appeared to be a large dog, standing near the bottom of the stony steps. He had no binoculars and he was too far away to make out any details, but he didn't want to go home yet and he was looking for an excuse to take a proper walk, so he decided to go on up and have a look.

23

Like a man pushing a car, Aengus put his shoulder to the pig's rump and heaved it up the last few metres of the final escarpment of the stony steps. They had reached the top at last, and the rest of the way to the beacon, about a quarter of a mile, would be level going.

Jenny flung her arms around Aengus's neck and kissed him on the cheek. 'You're the best daddy in the world!' she said.

'Can we let Mikey walk now?' said Donal. 'I mean, can we turn him back into himself?'

Aengus wiped the sweat from his brow and ignored the question. 'Is there anything to eat in that back-pack?' he said.

Donal reached into it and pulled out the paper bag that had contained the sandwiches. There was nothing in it apart from a few broken crusts and stray bits of cheese. Aengus shook his head, but the pig was not so fastidious. It snatched the bag from Donal's hand and ate it whole, with obvious relish.

Aengus sat down on a flat rock and watched it. 'Well,' he said, 'you can probably manage without me now, can you?'

'No we can't,' said Jenny. 'I'm frightened of the púca.'

'Two things you should know about púcas,' said Aengus. 'Always answer them politely and' – he looked sternly at Donal – 'never, but never, shake a stick at them.'

'Is that all?' said Jenny.

'Well, it's not quite all,' said Aengus. 'There are a few other things.'

At that moment JJ's head appeared over the edge of the escarpment.

'So that's where you two are,' he said to Jenny and Donal. He walked over to join them. 'Hello, Aengus,' he went on. 'I see you have a pig at last.'

'It's not a pig,' said Donal.

'I think it is,' said JJ. 'And a fine pig, too.'

He gave it a few hefty pats on the shoulder. It staggered and sat down with a grunt. JJ stepped away from it, quite pleased that he had not, after all, bought any cattle that day.

'Did you make me that fiddle yet?' said Aengus.

'You're joking!' said JJ. 'I've only had the wood for a few days.'

'Well, how was I supposed to know?' said Aengus grumpily. 'There's no logic to your world at all, as far as I can see.'

JJ sat on the limestone slab beside him. 'So what brings you here this time?'

Aengus gestured with a thumb towards Jenny, then his eyes widened with surprise and he turned to look. JJ turned, too. Where the pig had been, Mikey was now sitting, rubbing his bristly cheeks with both hands.

'Hello, Mikey,' said JJ. 'Where did you spring from?'

'Did you do that?' said Aengus to Jenny.

'I think so,' she said, looking pleased with herself.

'I've seen everything now,' said Mikey. 'Whoever would have thought there was so much brains in a pig? I'm sorry now I ever ate so many of them.'

'What are you doing up here, Mikey?' said JJ.

'I've come up to stand on the beacon,' he said. 'I love the way the world looks from up there. Help me up now, and let's finish what we started.'

JJ stood and helped him up and then stepped closer and got a grip under his left arm and elbow.

'There's no need for that,' said Mikey. 'I'm well able to walk on my own!' He took his stick from Donal. 'Let go of me now!'

'I will not,' said JJ. 'The ground up here is very

rough and I'm not prepared to carry you back down if you break your knee or your ankle.'

'No one's going to carry me anywhere,' said Mikey, but he submitted to JJ's support and the little group began making rapid progress. But they didn't get far. Up from the blind side of the hill came the púca and, as he had done before, he planted himself directly in their way.

For a moment Jenny didn't understand. Why would the púca come back and try again when he knew that Aengus was with them? Then she saw movement away to her right and looked. The edge of the mountain was swarming with goats.

JJ saw them, too. They were a motley crew; black and brown and tawny and piebald and white. There were craggy old nannies and elegant young does, big bearded pucks and a scatter of half-grown kids. JJ had been observing herds like this all his life. Surely they were just ordinary goats? They couldn't all be púcas, could they?

Aengus answered the question for him. 'Uh-oh. Looks like a bit more than I can handle.' He grinned sheepishly at JJ, took a step to his left and vanished into the hilltop.

'I thought I'd seen everything,' said Mikey. 'I have now.'

The goats ranged themselves in a rough semicircle,

not taking part in the stand-off but watching with obvious interest.

'You've had your little jaunt, now,' said the púca. 'Well done. You got the pig to the top of the hill and now you can take him back down again.' He advanced a few steps, tossing his dangerous horns.

'I think we'd better go back,' said Donal. 'Don't you, Mikey?'

Mikey didn't answer, but Jenny did. 'We're not going back. Not until we've got Mikey to the top of the beacon.'

She was thinking hard. She knew she had one trump card left in her hand and she had to work out the best way to play it. Then it came to her and, without a word to anyone, she began to walk towards the púca.

'Jenny!' JJ snapped. 'Stay where you are!'

She ignored him and he raced after her and grabbed her by the arm. Jenny spun round to face him and yanked herself free of his grip.

'For once in your life will you do as you're told!' said JJ. He reached out and tried to take hold of her again and, without a moment's hesitation, she turned him into a pig.

'Would you look at that?' said Mikey. 'And she only eleven years old!'

Jenny's eyes were blazing with anger as she confronted the púca. 'Are you deliberately trying to ruin everything or are you just as stupid as you look?'

The púca stood his ground and stared at her through those hard, unsettling eyes.

'Don't you realize the ghost can see you?' she went on. 'You and all your cronies? You're ruining everything I've done. He'll smell a rat when he sees you and he'll never believe another word I say.'

The púca glanced over his shoulder at the beacon and then turned back to Jenny.

'You can't make a deal with someone and then just go and sabotage it!' she said, still speaking angrily. 'I've already started to keep my side of it. The ghost is weaker. You know he is.'

Still the púca said nothing, but continued to gaze at her with an inscrutable expression.

'I was going to talk to him again today but I can't if you won't let me through.'

The púca looked over her shoulder at the others but Jenny didn't turn. She could hear the pig snuffling around behind her, probably grubbing up worms or roots.

'Why did you bring half the county with you, then?' asked the púca.

'Because the ghost loves company. I wanted to give him a proper send-off.'

'I don't want that old man on the beacon,' said the púca.

'Why not?' said Jenny. 'What do you think he can do?'

'He's the High King,' said the púca.

'So what if he is?' said Jenny. 'He's just an ancient ploddy. He doesn't have any power.'

She waited. The púca neither moved nor spoke.

'It's up to you,' said Jenny at last. 'If you let me through I'll have that ghost out of there before the end of the day. But I'm not going anywhere without the others. I'm not going to disappoint Mikey now he's come all this way.'

Still the púca said nothing, but he swished his tail and shifted restlessly from foot to foot.

'Well?' said Jenny. 'Do we have a deal or don't we?'

24

Despite what they thought, Aengus Óg had not abandoned Jenny and the others. He had, in fact, dropped back into Tír na n'Óg to try and get a bit of help from his father, the king of the fairies.

On this side of the time skin the world looked very similar to the way it did on the other, although the sun was a little further towards the west. Aengus and the Dagda stood on the flat mountain top beside a pile of stones that resembled, in most respects, the one on Sliabh Carron. But there were slight differences. This one looked fresher, as if it had just been built, and there was no grass growing on the sides. And it didn't have a hatchet buried underneath it either, or a ghost guarding it. It was there for an entirely different reason.

Aengus explained to the Dagda about Jenny and Mikey and their trip up the mountain and the resistance they were meeting from the púcas.

'Why would you concern yourself with that?' said the Dagda, swinging a fold of his heavy cape dramatically over his shoulder. 'It's ploddy business. Nothing to do with us.'

'But it's my daughter, you see,' said Aengus. 'I promised to help her if she asked me to. I never thought she would, of course. But she did.'

'And since when have promises been so important to you? I don't recall you ever keeping one before.'

Now that he thought about it, Aengus wondered if his father wasn't right.

'You can't go running around after them every time they don't get their own way,' the Dagda went on. 'It's easy to spoil children, you know, and not at all easy to unspoil them.'

'But there's definitely something fishy going on,' said Aengus. 'You know that white púca? The one that sometimes hangs around here in the woods?'

'I do,' said the Dagda.

'Well, he stole a chiming maple from the bottom of the hill. Just put in his hand and took it without a please or a thank you. And now the same one is up there getting in everyone's way.'

'I'm sure he has his reasons,' said the Dagda. 'On reflection I'm not at all sure I did the right thing when I persuaded them to bury the hatchet with the ploddies.'

' "Persuaded" is good,' said Aengus quietly.

'What?'

'Nothing, Father. Do go on.'

'Well, it's just that the ploddies have made such a dog's dinner of the place. I'm not sure we shouldn't have left the púcas to do as they pleased.'

Aengus found it hard to disagree with this as well. The land of the ploddies had changed an awful lot since he grew up in it. He didn't mind going over for a visit now and then but he wouldn't have wanted to live there.

'Anyway,' the Dagda went on, 'they're not our concern now. Let their new god sort it out for them, if he can.'

'You're probably right, Dad,' said Aengus. 'I probably shouldn't interfere.'

'You probably shouldn't,' said the Dagda. 'But you probably will.'

25

The púca moved out of Jenny's way and she turned the pig back into JJ. He retrieved his fiddle case and checked that there were no signs of damage, then strode up beside Jenny.

'Don't you ever, ever, ever do that again,' he said, in the best angry-father voice he could manage. When his words met with nothing better than a cold shoulder he decided to take a slightly less authoritarian approach.

'Please?'

Jenny promised, and the two of them stopped and waited for Donal and Mikey to catch up. Behind them the goats had regrouped and were standing together at the top of the stony steps, watching intently.

It wasn't far now to the beacon, and there were no further obstacles apart from the low stone wall which separated the Liddy winterage from Mikey's, and which JJ demolished. Leaving the others to follow at

Mikey's pace, Jenny ran on ahead and scaled the beacon to talk to the ghost. She was shocked by how depressed he had become, and she realized how little effort would be required to fulfil her promise to the púca. But he perked up a little when she told him that the old man slowly making his way across the hilltop towards them was a distant relative of his. He told Jenny that he recognized Mikey and that he used to see him every day during the winters, although Mikey never saw him. He had missed him when he stopped coming up here, and he thought he must have died.

They chatted on about the brevity of human existence and the longevity of ghosts until, eventually, the rest of the party made it to the foot of the beacon. Mikey was looking very tired and JJ, clearly worried about him, tried to get him to sit down at the bottom. But Mikey was determined to get to the top and, with a lot of assistance from JJ, he finally made it. Then he stood at the highest point, trembling and fighting for breath, and gazed out over the plain towards the sea.

'I made it,' he gasped. 'And fair play to the lot of ye for helping me do it.'

JJ was shaking his head distractedly. 'I don't know what you were thinking of, Mikey. And I don't know what these two were thinking of, either, egging you on.'

'I'll sit down now,' said Mikey. 'Give me your hand.'

JJ and Donal helped him to the nearest patch of grass and took his weight between them as his knees buckled. They got him sitting down but he didn't seem to have the strength to keep his head up, and JJ eased him gently into a lying position with his head nearly at the top of the beacon.

Donal took his hand. 'Mikey?' he said.

'Don't worry, Donal,' said Mikey. 'I'm exactly where I want to be.' But his voice was very frail, and Donal was very worried indeed. So was JJ.

'I think I'm going to call the air-sea rescue,' he said. He patted each of his pockets several times before he remembered that he had left his mobile phone, quite deliberately, on the kitchen table at home.

It was, along with Aisling's reading glasses, Donal's gamepod and a framed photograph of Helen and Ciaran, getting a really good wash, in about five litres of extremely sudsy water.

Aisling was wandering the house searching for the same glasses. She looked at her watch and wondered where everyone had got to. Hazel had told her she hadn't seen Donal or Jenny all day. That wasn't unusual for Jenny, but Donal was more considerate and generally let someone know what his plans were. She rang JJ's mobile, only to be informed that the person whose number she was calling was unavailable.

Slamming the phone down, she went into the kitchen and looked out of the window to check on Aidan. He, at least, was as happy as Larry, up to his armpits in his washing-up bucket. Aisling smiled a fond smile and resumed the hunt for her specs.

Mikey's lips were blue and his breathing was rapid and shallow.

'Donal,' said JJ. 'Run down to the house, will you, and get your mother to phone for the air-sea rescue.'

But Mikey shook his head and tightened his grip on Donal's hand. 'Don't anybody go anywhere,' he said, his voice faint but clear. 'I want you all with me now.'

At the top of the beacon, not far from Mikey's head, Jenny was watching and talking, quietly but urgently, to the ghost. And the ghost, listening, was gradually losing his grip on the earth. He was getting ready to leave and, out on the rim of the mountain top, the gathered púcas sensed how fast he was weakening and began to close in.

'You did the right thing, Donal,' Mikey was saying. 'Don't ever let anyone tell you any different.'

'You'll be OK, Mikey,' said Donal, fighting back tears.

'I will,' said Mikey. 'And very soon, too.'

The ghost was drifting, his vague form curling like smoke in the corner of Jenny's vision.

'I have a promise to make,' said Mikey. 'But you have to make one first, Donal. A promise to me.'

'I will,' said Donal. 'Anything you want.'

'You've to come up here every single day of the winter and stand up here on the beacon. And then you've to go on and cast your eye over your cattle.'

Donal was in tears now. He glanced at JJ, convinced that Mikey was raving. But JJ just nodded, and Donal managed to get the words out.

'I will, Mikey. I promise you I will.'

The ghost was in the air above the beacon; still attached to it, but only just. The púcas, swelling as they came, were racing across the grassland with terrifying speed. Jenny watched them, her heart in her mouth.

'And now for my promise,' said Mikey.

His voice was so weak that Donal and JJ had to lean close to hear. 'I swear that I will stand guard over this place . . .'

The advancing beasts could be heard now, their colossal feet shaking the rock beneath the thin soil. JJ looked up and saw them coming, but Donal kept his face beside Mikey's, and only he heard the very last words he said.

'. . . whether I am alive or dead.'

The ghost lifted high into the air and, with a crash like an air strike, the goat-gods hit the beacon. Staring out in horror, like woodlice on a burning log, JJ and Jenny saw the huge, reptilian eyes on a level with their own. The púcas could have swallowed them whole with their huge, fang-lined jaws, but they were still on their honour. Until they unearthed the hatchet they could not harm people, and so they didn't. The beacon shook, then began to subside as they gouged at the stones, each of their clawed fists tearing out a lorry-load at a time.

JJ was thrown off the side and ran clear between the huge, scaly thighs of the raging gods. Jenny clung on, thrown from rock to shifting rock. Donal's wails of terror rose above the sound of crashing rocks. Beneath him the whole structure was heaving and collapsing, but in all the turmoil he never once let go of Mikey's hand. He stayed crouched beside him right to the end, and when that end came, he was the only one to see the light in the old man's eyes finally go out.

But everyone felt the effect. It was instantaneous and extraordinary. The destruction of the beacon stopped. Hissing and snorting, the púcas flung them-selves clear of it and, resuming their goat shapes, they raced away from it as fast as they could.

26

Down in the Liddy house, Aisling was sorting through the waste-paper basket, still looking for her glasses, when Aidan hurled himself against the back door and burst into the kitchen.

'A big herring!' he squawked at her. He was soaked from head to foot, and covered with soapy bubbles.

'Really?' said Aisling absently.

'A huge big herring,' said Aidan, clutching her hand and hauling her towards the door.

The first thing Aisling saw was an enormous white bird climbing steeply into the sky. It wasn't a herring, and nor was it a heron, which was what Aidan had meant. Though she had never seen one before, Aisling was absolutely certain that it was a stork.

And it had brought, she now saw, what it is that storks bring. At her feet, wrapped in a very familiar yellow shawl, was a baby. Aisling bent and picked it

305

up, instantly recognizing its tiny features and its very own sweet smell.

'It's a baby!' yelled Aidan excitedly.

'Yes, it is,' said Aisling, suddenly blinded by tears. 'It's a beautiful little baby girl, and the stork brought her just for us.'

'Look!' said Jenny.

Donal and JJ, still watching the retreating goats, thought they were already looking, but Jenny was seeing something else. She was facing west but pointing north and, since Donal knew what that meant, he looked west as well. On the edge of his vision he saw a small grey cloud, spangled by tiny points of light. Then he saw that there was a second one, arriving from the direction of the plain and moving in to meet the first.

'Two of them?' he said to Jenny.

'Two what?' said JJ, who had never figured out how to look.

'The other one is the ghost from Mikey's fort,' said Jenny.

'How do you know?' Donal asked.

'Because I talked to it. Do you know who it is?'

'Who what is?' said JJ, picking his way over the sprawl of strewn rocks that had once been the beacon.

'It's the boy ghost's dad,' said Jenny. 'The first High King of Ireland.'

'What is?' said JJ.

'He made a dying vow as well,' Jenny went on. 'He swore he would never leave the earth as long as his son was still bound to it. And he didn't.'

'So that was what those conversations were all about,' said Donal. 'He was trying to persuade Mikey to come and take his son's place.'

'I don't think Mikey needed much persuading,' said Jenny. 'Can you see him there now?'

Donal shifted his gaze until he caught sight of the new ghost, much stronger and clearer than the last one, standing on top of what remained of the beacon.

'Look, Dad,' said Donal.

JJ looked, all wrong, and Donal explained how to do it properly. On the third attempt, JJ finally succeeded, and his face softened with delight. He couldn't see any features, just the figure's outline, but he could feel Mikey's fierce joy at being there, looking out over the high place that he had loved all his life.

Jenny looked off into the distance and saw the white goat standing in the distance, alone again now. She wondered whether he had delivered the baby and suddenly, unexpectedly, she felt a pang of deep regret about what she had done. She had kept her side of the deal but, true to her kind, she had tricked him as well. It had been touch and go for a while there, and she had been afraid it wasn't going to work, but it had, and the hatchet remained safely buried. So the human race was still free to go about destroying the beautiful planet that the púcas had made.

And whether they deserved that or not was for greater gods than Jenny to decide.

27

'Why don't you play him a tune, JJ? He'd like that, wouldn't you, Mikey?'

They all turned towards the voice and saw Aengus Óg standing among the rubble.

'I seem to have missed the best bit,' he said. 'What happened?'

Nobody bothered to fill him in, and he climbed carefully up the unstable side of the beacon and looked down at Mikey's body.

'Another one gone,' he said. 'That's ploddies for you. Here today and gone tomorrow.'

Donal finally let go of Mikey's hand. He thought he ought to feel sad, but he couldn't. He knew Mikey was still there, watching them, far happier now that he was no longer tied to this painful old body.

'Was it those old goats made all this mess?' said Aengus.

'Yes,' said JJ, looking around at the devastation. 'I

suppose at some stage we'll have to think about trying to rebuild it. Quite an undertaking, though.'

'Oh, my dad can fix that,' said Aengus glibly.

'Really?' said JJ.

'Listen,' said Aengus. 'My dad can fix anything. He could have put Humpty Dumpty together again if anyone had thought to ask him.'

'That's great,' said JJ. 'But first things first. We'd better see about getting Mikey down off this mountain. Will you go down to the house now, Donal?'

'What about the púca?' said Donal.

'If he gives you any trouble you tell him I'm watching,' said Aengus. 'Tell him I'll turn him into a poodle and give him to your little brother as a Christmas present. That'll soon shut him up.'

Donal ran off and Aengus went on: 'I meant it, JJ. About playing a tune for Mikey. To send him on his way.'

'But he isn't going anywhere,' said JJ. 'He's just there, see?'

'All the more reason, then,' said Aengus, and it was hard for JJ to argue with logic like that. So he took out the neglected Stradivarius and played a slow air, and even though the strings were past their best the old fiddle pulled pure emotion out of the ether and turned it into sound. The tune was so beautiful that it brought the Dagda through the time skin, as Aengus had known it would, and the Dagda was so delighted with JJ's playing that he cleared everybody out of the way and repaired the beacon there and then, as Aengus had very much hoped he would.

Donal arrived home to discover Hazel walking up and down the kitchen trying to comfort a fretful baby.

'Where did that come from?' he asked. 'I thought you weren't going to have a baby.'

'Well, I am,' said Hazel. 'The stork brought it.'

Aisling had gone out to get goat's milk and feeding bottles. So it was Hazel who made the 999 call when Donal told her what had happened. As soon as they were sure that help was on its way, Donal decided to walk down and tell Nancy McGrath that Mikey was dead.

'Not a word about the baby,' said Hazel. 'And don't let her come round here gossiping!'

It was all suddenly way too much for a nine-year-old to handle, and Donal dropped into the armchair and began to cry. Hazel put an arm round him and hugged him until he felt better, then she handed him the baby and made the phone call to Nancy McGrath herself.

* * *

JJ played some reels and some jigs, and then he played a hornpipe and the Dagda danced to it on the topmost stone of the beacon. It was the most manly and yet the most graceful dancing that JJ had ever seen, and he felt honoured to have had the privilege of playing for it. And all the time Mikey's corpse lay at the foot of the beacon and stared up at the sky, but Mikey's ghost missed nothing, and the tunes and the dancing went on until Jenny spotted the black speck of the helicopter in the distance, coming across Galway Bay.

'We'd best be off then,' said Aengus Óg.

'I suppose you'd better,' said JJ.

'Come and visit us soon,' said Aengus. 'And don't forget you promised to make me a fiddle.'

'I will,' said JJ, 'and I won't.'

He bent to put the Stradivarius away in its case, and when he looked up again they were gone.

All of them.

'Jenny?' JJ said, looking around. 'Jenny?'

But there was no answer. The fairy child had gone, along with her father and her grandfather, to the land of eternal youth.

28

There was one more thing that Donal had to do, because Mikey's old dog, Belle, was still shut in the house waiting for him to come home. Someone was going to have to look after her. So he walked down to the house, but when he arrived there he found that it wasn't empty. Nancy McGrath had got there before him, and Belle was tucking into a bowl of meat and biscuits.

Nancy's eyes were swollen from crying. 'I can't believe he's gone,' she said. 'They broke the mould when they made Mikey.'

Donal nodded, struggling with tears again.

'Would you like to keep the dog?' said Nancy. 'Mikey would have wanted you to have her.'

Donal nodded again. Hazel would be delighted. Aidan would, too, for different reasons, but he would just have to learn to be nice to her.

'He thought the world of you, Donal,' Nancy went

on. 'I probably shouldn't tell you this before the will is read, but I know it's the truth so I will. He left the house to me, and the home farm here. But he left the winterage to you.'

'To me?'

Donal looked out of the window at the mountain. So Mikey hadn't been raving after all. Resolve flooded into Donal's heart. He would keep his promise and go up there every day of the winter. He would stand on the beacon and talk to Mikey's ghost, and then he would walk the mountain top, checking on his cattle.

'I suppose we should tidy up a bit,' said Nancy, looking around the room. 'They'll bring him back here tomorrow, won't they? For the wake? The whole of the county will want to come and pay their last respects.'

Donal went over to the fireplace and began to poke at the deep pile of ashes.

'You may as well let that go out,' said Nancy. 'There's no need for it now.'

But Donal continued to rake through the ashes. There wasn't a single glowing ember, not even a spark. The fire of the High Kings, which had burned continuously for three thousand years, had finally let itself out.

29

The police had accompanied the rescue team and the scene of Mikey's death had been carefully examined and photographed. After that the body had been loaded into the aircraft and JJ was aware of the ghost looking on, enjoying this final irony. Mikey was getting his helicopter ride at last, but down the mountain instead of up it.

JJ accompanied him to the morgue, then went to the police station to give a full statement. The officers were stern and punctilious. They told him that taking Mikey up the mountain had been irresponsible, but it wasn't criminal, and JJ was certain that they didn't suspect him of foul play.

It was several hours later and night had fallen before JJ arrived home. When he got into the house the first thing he saw was the baby, sleeping peacefully in a cardboard box beside the range. JJ stared at it in amazement, and Aisling told him how it came to be there. Then JJ told her that Jenny had gone back to Tír na n'Óg, and the strange thing was that even though this had been what they both wanted, neither of them was happy.

'I suppose it's back to plan A, then,' said Aisling eventually. 'We'd better phone Helen and Ciaran and let them know.'

JJ nodded.

'And I suppose we'd better phone the guards and tell them Jenny is missing.'

But this time JJ shook his head. 'No,' he said. 'Not that bit. Not yet.'

SEPTEMBER

1

JJ finished playing the set of reels and watched the dancers separate and drift away to retrieve their drinks. He didn't much like the fiddle he was playing and he wondered, for the umpteenth time, why he hadn't brought his own one. There had been a good reason for it, he was sure, but no matter how hard he tried he couldn't remember what it was.

He glanced around at the other musicians. Devaney was there with his bodhrán, and Drowsy Maggie and Aengus with their fiddles, and the flute player and the whistle player, whose names now he couldn't remember. It was a long, long time since he had last played with them. It was for him, anyway. He had assimilated the fairy rhythms and intonations pretty well on that last visit, but he was delighted to be getting a refresher course, and to be reminded of some of the old tunes that he had forgotten. He couldn't remember when he had last enjoyed a tune so much. But then, he couldn't remember very much at all.

Anne Korff and her little dog Lottie were standing looking out to sea, and nearby, on the wall of the tiny harbour, Donal and Jenny were sitting together. JJ had been watching them. They were clearly enjoying the music and they both tapped their feet along to the beat, but neither of them had been tempted to dance yet. JJ had seen several people chatting to them and holding out their hands in invitation, but the children shook their heads and looked away, and returned to the quiet enjoyment of each other's company.

'Did you make that fiddle for me yet, JJ?'

'What fiddle?' said JJ.

Aengus grinned at his ploddy grandson and tuned his instrument. It needed new strings, JJ noticed. In fact, all the fiddles did. Next time he came he would bring some.

If he remembered.

'Do you know "The Old Grey Goose"?' said Aengus.

'Of course I do,' said JJ, and he was just starting into the famous old jig when he felt a tap on the shoulder. He turned round to see Séadna Tobín standing on the footpath behind him.

'Time to go home, JJ,' he said.

'Really?' said JJ. 'Already? But I only just got here.'

'All the same,' said Séadna, 'it's time to go.'

'Grand,' said JJ, bitterly disappointed. 'I'll just play this last tune.'

'Better if you didn't,' said Séadna.

JJ stood up and offered the fiddle to him. 'Play it yourself, then,' he said. "The Old Grey Goose". You know that one.'

But Séadna stood with his arms folded and shook his head firmly.

'Ah, don't mind him,' said Devaney dismissively. 'He's just an old stuffed shirt.'

JJ would love to have bought that, but he just couldn't. The Kinvara pharmacist was many things but a stuffed shirt wasn't one of them. Reluctantly he put his fiddle down and walked across the road to the harbour wall.

'Time to go home, I'm afraid,' he said.

Donal stood up and dusted himself down. JJ glanced over at Séadna, then turned back to Jenny.

'Well, Jen?' he said. 'What do you think? Another few years with the Liddys?'

Jenny didn't look at him. She looked everywhere else: at the dancers laughing and flirting outside the pubs, at the golden light washing the distant mountains, at her parents sharing a joke with the other musicians on the opposite side of the road. Finally, visibly, she reached a decision. She got to her feet, smiled up at JJ, and took a good firm hold of his hand.

Glossary

'Black dot' accordion – A hohner instrument that has a keyboard of white buttons with a single black one

Bodhrán – A traditional Irish drum made from goatskin

Céilí – A dance

Garda – Police/Irish policeman

Gardai/guards – The Irish police

Grike – A crack, often very deep, found in limestone bedrock

Haggard – A small enclosure beside a farmhouse

Hornpipe – A dance tune also in 4/4 time but with a distinctively different rhythm to a reel

Hurling – A very old and very fast game played with ash sticks and a hard ball

Jig – A dance tune in 6/8 time. A slip jig is in 9/8 time

Púca – A mythical creature which appears in the form of a goat

Reel – A dance tune in 4/4 time

Set dance – a dance with eight people, which has a number of different parts

Souterrain – An underground chamber or series of chambers, commonly found in ancient Irish ring forts

Winterage – An area of land, often rough, used by farmers for winter grazing. Winterage in the Burren area is particularly prized as it will sustain cattle throughout the winter without the need for supplemental feeding

Bibliography

Lady Augusta Gregory, *Gods and Fighting Men* (Kessinger Publishing Co., 2004)

— *Cuchulain of Muirthemne* (Dover Publications, 2001)

— *Visions and Beliefs in the West of Ireland* (Colin Smythe Ltd, 1976)

James Stephens, *Irish Fairy Tales* (Lightning Source UK Ltd, 2004)

Lady Wilde, *Ancient Legends, Mystic Charms and Superstitions of Ireland* (1925; reprinted: Lemma Publishing Corporation, New York, 1973)

Turn over to read the beginning of
The New Policeman, which tells how fifteen-year-old
JJ sets out to try and buy his mother some time, and
finds out some truly remarkable things about music,
myth and magic along the way.

1

JJ Liddy and his best friend Jimmy Dowling often had arguments. JJ never took them seriously. He even considered them a sign of the strength of the friendship, because they always made up again straight away, unlike some of the girls in school, who got into major possessive battles with each other. But on that day in early September, during the first week that they were back in school, they had an argument like none before.

JJ couldn't even remember now what it had been about. But at the end of it, at the point where they usually came round to forgiving each other and patching it up, Jimmy had dropped a bombshell.

'I should have had more sense than to hang around with you anyway, after what my granny told me about the Liddys.'

His words were followed by a dreadful silence, full of JJ's bewilderment and Jimmy's embarrassment. He knew he had gone too far.

'What about the Liddys?' said JJ.

'Nothing.' Jimmy turned to go back into school.

JJ stood in front of him. 'Go on. What did she tell you?'

Jimmy might have been able to wriggle his way out of it and pretend it was a bluff, but he had been overheard. He and JJ were no longer alone. Two other lads, Aidan Currie and Mike Ford, had overheard and had come to join in.

'Go on, Jimmy,' said Aidan. 'You may as well tell him.'

'Yeah,' said Mike. 'If he doesn't know he must be the only person in the county who doesn't.'

The bell rang for the end of the morning break. They all ignored it.

'Know what?' said JJ. He felt cold, terrified, not of something that might happen but of something that he might find inside himself; in his blood.

'It was a long time ago,' said Jimmy, still trying to retract.

'What was?'

'One of the Liddys . . .' Jimmy said something else but he mumbled it beneath his breath and JJ couldn't hear. It sounded like 'burgled the beast'.

The teacher on yard duty was calling them in. Jimmy began to walk towards the school. The others fell in.

'He did what?' said JJ.

'Forget it,' said Jimmy.

It was Aidan Currie who said it, loud enough for JJ or anyone else to hear. 'Sure everyone knows about it. Your great-granddad. JJ Liddy, same as yourself. He murdered the priest.'

JJ stopped in his tracks. 'No way!'

'He did, so,' said Mike. 'And all for the sake of an old wooden flute.'

'You're a shower of liars!' said JJ.

The boys, except for Jimmy, laughed.

'Always mad for the music, the same Liddys,' said Mike.

He began to hop and skip towards the school in a goofy parody of Irish dancing. Aidan trotted beside him, singing an out-of-tune version of 'The Irish Washerwoman'. Jimmy glanced back at JJ and, his head down, followed them as they went back in.

JJ stood alone in the yard. It couldn't be true. But he knew, now that he thought about it, that there had always been something behind the way some of the local people regarded him and his family. A lot of people in the community came to the céilís and the set-dancing classes that were held at his house on Saturdays. They had always come, and their parents and grandparents had come before them. In recent years the numbers had increased dramatically with the influx of new people into the area. Some of them came from thirty miles away and more. But there was, and always had been, a large number of local people who would have nothing to do with the Liddys or their music. They didn't exactly cross the street to avoid JJ and his family, but they didn't talk to them either. JJ, if he'd thought about it at all, had assumed it was because his parents were one of the only couples in the district who weren't married, but what if that wasn't the reason? What if it had really happened? Could JJ be descended from a murderer?

'Liddy!'

The teacher was standing at the door, waiting for him.

JJ hesitated. For a moment it seemed to him that there was no way he could set foot inside that school again. Then the solution came to him.

The teacher closed the door behind him. 'What do you think you were doing, standing out there like a lemon?'

'Sorry,' said JJ. 'I didn't realize you were talking to me.'

'Who else would I be talking to?'

'My name's Byrne,' said JJ. 'My mother's name is Liddy all right, but my father's name is Byrne. I'm JJ Byrne.'

THE LEGACY

Trad

2

The new policeman stood on the street outside Green's pub. On the other side of the bolted doors a gathering of musicians was at full throttle, the rich blend of their instruments cutting through the beehive buzz of a dozen conversations. Across the road the rising tide slopped against the walls of the tiny harbour. Beneath invisible clouds the water was pewter-grey with muddy bronze glints where it caught the street lights. Its surface was ragged. The breeze was getting up. There would be rain before long.

Inside the pub there was a momentary hiccup in the music as one tune ended and another began. For a couple of bars a solitary flute carried the new tune until the other musicians recognized it and pounced on it, and lifted it to the rafters of the old pub. Out in the street, Garda O'Dwyer recognized the tune. Inside his regulation black brogues his cramped toes twitched to the beat. At the kerbside behind him his partner, Garda Treacy, leaned across the empty passenger seat of the squad car and tapped on the window.

Larry O'Dwyer sighed and took a step towards the

narrow double doors. He'd had a good reason for becoming a policeman but sometimes it was difficult to remember what it was. It wasn't this; he was sure of that much. He hadn't become a policeman to curtail the enjoyment of musicians and their audiences. A few miles away, in Galway city, violent crime was escalating dramatically. Street gangs were engaged in all kinds of thuggery and muggery. He would be of far more use to society there. But that, as far as he could remember, was not why he had become a policeman either. There were times, like now, when he suspected that the reason, whatever it was, might not have been a particularly good one.

The tune changed again. The light inside the squad car came on as Garda Treacy opened his door. Larry stilled his tapping foot and rapped with his knuckles on Mary Green's door.

Inside the pub throats closed, conversations collapsed, the drone of voices faltered and died. One by one the musicians dropped out of the tune, leaving, for a while, an oblivious fiddler tearing away enthusiastically on her own. Someone got through to her finally, and the music stopped mid-bar. The only sound that followed was Mary Green's light footsteps crossing the concrete floor.

One of the narrow doors opened a crack. Mary's anxious face appeared. Behind her, Larry could see

Anne Korff perched on a bar stool. She was one of the few people in the village that he had already met. He hoped he would not be required to take her name.

'I'm sorry, now,' he said to Mary Green. 'It's a quarter to one.'

'They're just finishing up,' said Mary earnestly. 'They'll be gone in five minutes.'

'I hope so,' said Larry. 'That would be the best thing for everyone.'

As he returned to the car, the first drops of rain were beginning to fall on to the surface of the sea.

THE NEW POLICEMAN

Trad

3

They were falling, as well, on JJ Liddy – or JJ Byrne, as he now called himself. They were falling on his father Ciaran, and on the last few bales of hay that they were loading on to the flat-bed trailer in the Ring Field; the highest meadow on their land.

'How's that for timing?' said Ciaran.

JJ didn't answer. He was too tired to answer. Inside his gloves his fingers were red raw from the hundreds of bale strings that had been through his hands that evening. He threw up the last bale. Ciaran stacked it neatly and dropped down into the tractor seat. JJ helped Bosco up into the cab beside him. The dog was too old and stiff now to jump up on his own, but he wasn't too old to want to be part of everything that was happening on the farm. Wherever there was work being done, there was Bosco.

Ciaran let in the clutch and the old tractor began to rumble and clunk across the new-mown meadow. JJ climbed up on top of the bales. The rain was falling more heavily now. Drops slanted across the headlight beam as they skirted the ring fort and emerged on

341

to the rutted track which led down to the farmyard.

Ciaran was right. It was good timing. The hay they had just saved was a late crop; almost an afterthought. The summer had been wet, and their previous attempts at hay-making had been disastrous. In the end they had brought in contractors to wrap what was left of their crop in round black bales. It had been too wet to be hay but not fresh enough to be silage. They called the resulting hybrid haylage, but it was optimistic. Even if the stock were hungry enough to eat it they wouldn't get a great deal of nutrition from it. This crop was good, and it would make up some of the fodder shortfall, but by no means all of it. Farming was a tough station.

The trailer lurched. In the cab ahead of him, JJ could see Bosco's tail waving about as he was thrown from side to side. To their right, on the other side of the electric fence, was Molly's Place; the field behind the house which the Liddys had called after some long-forgotten donkey. A stream of mottled shapes was moving across it now, like a school of fish gliding through the black depths of the sea. The goats – white Saanens and brown-and-white Toggenburgs – were heading for their shelter at the edge of the yard.

Goats hated rain. So did JJ. Now that he had stopped working, his body temperature had plummeted. Drops were rolling out of his hair and stinging his eyes. He longed for his bed.

Ciaran swung the tractor round in the yard. 'We'll unload in the morning.'

JJ nodded, hopped down from the bales and semaphored to Ciaran as he reversed the trailer into the empty bay of the hay shed. His mother, Helen, emerged from the back door and came over.

'Brilliant timing,' she said. 'Tea's just made.'

But JJ walked straight past the pot, which steamed on the range in the kitchen, and the plates of fresh scones on the table. Upstairs in his room his school bag lay open on his bed, leaking overdue homework. He glanced at the clock. If he got up half an hour early the next morning he could get a bit of it done.

He spilled the bag and its contents on to the floor, and as he set the alarm he wondered, as he wondered every day, where on earth all the time went.

THE NEW-MOWN
MEADOW

Trad

4

It wasn't that Mary Green didn't want her customers to leave. The bar was firmly closed and she had been pleading with them all to go since the new policeman had knocked. Most of her regulars had drunk up and gone, but not all. Some of the musicians were from out of town, and this was one of the best sessions they had played in for years. Their fingers, their bows, their breath – the instruments themselves, it seemed – had all been taken over by the spirit of that wild, anarchic music. They wanted to oblige Mary, who was pacing the floor and wringing her hands in anxiety, but they just couldn't. Tunes they hadn't heard for years kept popping into their heads and demanding to be played. It was always like that in Green's. There was just something about the place.

It was 1.30 a.m. Outside in the street, Garda Larry O'Dwyer was standing in the pouring rain, paralysed by the beauty of the music behind Mary's blackout curtains. But this time Garda Treacy was at his side and ready to go in.

'Bad luck to stop them in the middle of a tune,' said

Larry, but Treacy was already pounding on the door.

Mary opened it. 'They're going,' she said. 'They're packed up and all.'

The two guards edged past her just in time to catch a glimpse of a pair of heels and a fiddle case disappearing out of the back door. Larry knew he'd seen them before. He also knew how pointless it would be to try and remember where. Before anyone else could slip out the same way Garda Treacy crossed the pub floor and stood beside the back door, taking out his notebook on the way. All the tables, even the ones surrounded by musicians, were clear and tidy. It was music, not drink, that had kept the crowd where they were. Nonetheless, they were all breaking the law.

Garda Treacy began to take the names of the musicians. Larry pulled out his notebook.

'There's no need,' said Mary Green helplessly. 'They're all going now.'

Anne Korff was sitting where Larry had last seen her, on a bar stool beside the street door. He opened the notebook and took the lid off his pen.

'Name?'

'Er . . . Lucy Campbell,' said Anne Korff, in a distinct German accent.

'Lucy Campbell,' said Larry, fixing her with what he intended to be a hard stare.

She subdued the smile still wriggling at the corners of her mouth. 'That's right. Lucy. L-U-C—'

Larry sighed. 'I know how to spell it.' He wrote it down. There was little else he could do. He knew what her real name was. But then, she knew what his real name was as well.

LUCY CAMPBELL

Traditional

5

Helen was already out milking when JJ got up. There was a pot of tea on the table. He drank a cup as he tackled into the homework. By the time Helen came in again he had battled his way through the maths questions and was trying to get to grips with a history essay. Helen tiptoed around him, making fresh tea, putting out cereals and milk, slicing bread for the toaster, but he was aware of her eyes resting on the cover of his new maths copy. He thought for a moment that she might ignore it. She didn't.

'How come you're JJ Byrne all of a sudden?'

He put down his pen a bit too hard. 'Everyone in school uses their father's name. Why shouldn't I?'

'Because you're a Liddy,' said Helen. 'That's why.'

He could hear the tension in her voice. She didn't need to remind him of how important the name was to her, but she did it anyway. 'There have always been Liddys in this house. You know that. You know it's one of the reasons Ciaran and I didn't get married. So you and Marian would have my name. You're a Liddy, JJ. Ciaran doesn't mind, so why should you?'

JJ shrugged. 'I just want Dad's name, that's all.'

He knew she hadn't accepted it. She wouldn't, either. She left it, though, for the moment; put toast out on the table, spread butter on it while it was hot. There were other things she was due to find out about JJ and his relationship with the Liddy tradition, but he was in no hurry to cause more trouble. She would find out soon enough.

Ciaran came down, closely followed by JJ's younger sister, Marian. They were both appallingly bright and bubbly in the mornings, unlike him and his mother, who each took at least an hour to warm to the new day. Their breezy greetings were met with moody responses.

'Anything on after school today?' said Ciaran.

'Hurling training,' said JJ. 'Till half six.'

'I'll pick you up afterwards,' said Ciaran. 'I'll get the beer while I'm at it.'

JJ said nothing. The beer was for the céilí that the Liddys held on the second Saturday of every month; had held every second Saturday for generations. Helen played the concertina for the dancers and Phil Daly, a guitarist from the village, backed the tunes. For the last two years JJ had played with them, usually on the fiddle, sometimes on the flute as well.

'We never went over those tunes,' Helen was saying. 'I can't believe it's Friday already. Maybe we'll get a chance this evening?'

JJ reached for toast. He didn't need to say anything. They wouldn't go over the tunes that evening because that evening would be like every other; a mad race to pack in all the things that needed to be done.

'Is that the time?' said Ciaran.

They all turned to look at the clock. Ten minutes to eat breakfast and get to the bus. JJ snatched a mouthful of toast and began to stuff his school bag.